JUMP BALL

LAS VEGAS RAMBLERS

BOOK TWO

JUMP  BALL

LAS VEGAS RAMBLERS

BOOK TWO

Kasha Thompson

WEBSTER AVENUE PUBLISHING
SACRAMENTO, CA

JUMP BALL: LAS VEGAS RAMBLERS (BOOK 2)

Paperback ISBN: 979-8-9862679-4-4

Copyright 2024 Kasha Thompson

This edition published and arranged by Webster Avenue Publishing.

Printed in the United States of America. First Edition April 2024.

Character Illustration: Mary Rudkovskaya

Cover Design by: Webster Avenue Publishing

Interior Layout by: Webster Avenue Publishing

Editing: Courtney Driver of Whoproofedit.com

BLACK LOVE NOV·EL

/blak/ /ləv/ /nävə'

noun

1. a novel, with Black main characters that examines the complexity of falling and staying in love.

2. a story centered around Black love with just the right amount of sweet, savory, and spice.

CONTENT NOTES

Please note Jump Ball discusses topics which could potentially trigger certain audiences. Some readers may consider the following as spoilers.

Moderate coarse language
Several sexually explicit scenes
Death of a parent
Loss & grief
Physical disability

SARIAH

"Yes, just like that." I seeped in a breath of air, my hips rotating as I rode the face of the man I'd met at the hotel bar just hours before. Ho-ish? Yes. But what this man was doing to me was much needed after a stressful week in a foreign country. Plus, who doesn't travel to France and fuck a Frenchman? It's essentially a rite of passage. Granted this Frenchman's name was Roger, which was a huge disappointment. I was hoping I'd be screaming out the name Franz or Pierre, but Roger would have to do.

Right now, Roger's hands were planted on my waist and with an impressively long tongue, was satisfying my urgent need to bust a nut. My phone rang from its perch on the hotel night stand. Leaning forward, I fumbled for it, pressing the button declining the call, all the while never losing the connection between my lower lips and Frenchie's. Work brought me to Nice and I'd spent the week enjoying the food, shopping, and finally the men.

Roger lifted me from his face and asked, "I want to feel your pretty mouth around my dick. Will you?"

"Listen, if you make me come I'm liable to do just about anything you ask," I said, with an enthusiastic nod.

He clamped hold of my clit, working hard to hit my spot and I showed him how much I appreciated the effort by stroking his dick through his briefs. It wasn't big, but it had potential. My phone dinged several times, notifying me of incoming text messages. The dinging was followed by another call.

I grumbled under my breath, "Ugh, let me be great," before shutting my phone off all together.

It took a whole lot of concentration for me to get my head back into the game, but when I did, I quickly zoned out, writhing on top of Roger as the orgasm washed over me. I pressed my full weight on his head. Hopefully, he had good lung capacity because I didn't plan on releasing him until he'd sucked every last drop. With shaky legs, I collapsed onto the bed, still rubbing my nipples in a euphoric state.

Roger stood, pulling off his underwear. "I want you to choke on it," he said.

I looked at Roger, then at his dick and back again. I can assure you no one was choking on it.

"How do you say fuck me in French?" I asked. It was late and I didn't want to spend fifteen minutes with his pale peen in my mouth. I needed Roger to hit my spot and then bounce.

"Baise moi."

"Baise moi. I don't think I can wait any longer," I moaned, opening my legs wide in an attempt to really sell it. Roger took the bait and opted for a soft, warm place to land. Donning a condom, he sunk on top of me.

———

AFTER GETTING RID OF ROGER, I HEADED TO THE bathroom to take a shower. We had two more days in Nice and then we would close out our trip in Paris. I was traveling with my best friend and business partner, Tracie Kirk. We'd launched our makeup line, Genuine Beauty, ten years ago and were finally branching out into skincare. She and I were in France to show off our products to retailers for preorder.

Genuine Beauty was my baby. Since I was a young girl, I loved fashion and dressing up. When I turned sixteen, my mother finally allowed me to wear makeup. A little lip gloss or a dab of eye shadow. It was then I started to recognize the lack of products that complimented the deeper skin tones like my mahogany-hued skin. Genuine Beauty revolutionized the beauty industry by introducing a range of foundation shades and over a dozen nude-lip options that worked for more than just the lightest complexions. And we were about to shake the industry once again with our skincare line.

Piling my hair atop my head, I secured it under a shower cap. Before entering the shower, I turned my phone back on. I wanted to text Tracie so she could remind me what time we had to be out the door tomorrow morning. The information was written on my itinerary, which was somewhere under the mass of papers on the coffee table. Tracie was far better organized than me and I knew she would be able to provide the answer with little effort.

When my phone settled on the home screen after rebooting, I was inundated with text messages and missed calls from both my mother and Aunt Dina.

> Mom: Baby call me when you get this message.

> Mom: Sariah it's me again. Can you please call me back ASAP. It's urgent.

> Aunt Dina: Girl where are you at? Your mother is trying to reach you. Call us back.

> Mom: 911

There were several other text messages imploring me to contact them. I checked the last missed call. It was from my Aunt Dina. "Damnit Sariah, your father's had a heart attack and you can't even bother to answer your fucking phone. He's at Kaiser Hospital in Henderson. It doesn't look good. You need to get your ass back to Vegas."

I stared at my phone screen, frozen with shock. *Did Aunt Dina say it didn't look good?* What the hell did that mean? She didn't mean … she couldn't. My father was the strongest man I knew. Yes, he was seventy-two but he was the picture of health. He worked out every day, and he'd gone vegan after marrying Harper who, despite being with my father for ten years, was barely in her thirties.

I called Tracie. When she answered, I quickly blurted out, "My dad had a heart attack."

As if on cue, Tracie's mama bear instincts kicked in. "I'm on my way over."

In less than a minute, there was a knock on my hotel door. When I opened it, Tracie was standing there with wine and her laptop. Tracie's room was a few doors down from mine and it appeared she'd wasted no time grabbing the essentials and heading my way. "We need to book you a flight back home. I can help you pack your bags. Where is your luggage?"

I pointed toward the bedroom, sinking to the couch as she buzzed in and out of the suite's living quarters. She finally climbed into an armchair, crossing her legs. Opening her laptop, she started pulling up flights.

"Tracie," I whispered. "He's going to pull through, right?"

I knew Tracie's facial tics better than I knew my own. Her expression displayed a hint of concern but not alarm. "What did your mom say?"

"I don't know, I just opened my phone to a shit ton of messages and my Aunt Dina's voicemail saying it didn't look good."

"Let's just get you a flight. There's one leaving at six in the morning. It has a couple of layovers—"

"We have a ton of meetings tomorrow. I can't miss those."

"I can handle them." She stood, retrieving a glass from the bar and poured out some wine, handing it to me.

I slurped down the white wine, holding out my glass for more. "The last time we talked it ended in a fight."

"Don't do that. Don't you dare." She pointed a warning finger in my direction.

I was numb inside, disconnected from myself and what was happening around me. Crying would be helpful right about now, at least I would have a place to direct my energy, but I couldn't make the tears fall. I think my body went into self-preservation mode, cutting off my access to emotions so I didn't spiral. All I felt was confusion because nothing made sense. I knew I needed to call my mother but if I did, I would be able to hear the bleakness in her voice and it would confirm my aunt's words, "It doesn't look good."

Tracie managed to book a first-class flight back home. It would make two stops, Munich and then Denver. I'd land at McCarran airport in a little over seventeen hours. My father's driver, Mr. Charles, would pick me up from the airport. I was useless while I watched Tracie collect the items scattered across the living room and place them into my suitcase.

"How'd things go with the guy from the bar?" She was trying to distract me to stop my mind from descending to its lowest point.

"We had sex." My tone was dull and listless.

"Congratulations. At least one of us is getting some ass on this trip."

"What should I do?" I was in desperate need of direction.

"Get your passport and jewelry from the safe."

I stood, going through the motions as I tried to open

the hotel safe in my bedroom closet. "I can't remember the code," I called.

"It's Benji's birthday."

That's right, I always used my brother's birthday when I needed a numeric code. It probably wasn't the most secure password, but it was a date I knew by heart. Back in the living room, I handed Tracie the items I'd pulled from the safe and she stowed them away in my carry-on. Normally I was more helpful, but my brain was in a fog.

I touched my head and felt the plastic shower cap. "I need to shower."

"Good idea. A nice hot shower will do you good. While you do that, I'll finish packing the last few items."

The warm spray of the water did soothe my achy joints, which were sore from being at attention the past hour. Pulling my face under the water, I regulated my breaths, reminded of what my father always said. "Life isn't fair, there's no use in bitching and moaning about it." My dad believed he made his own destiny. Kind of progressive thinking from a man who was so grounded in reality. Life wasn't what happened to you. It was how you moved through it. One thing my father wasn't afraid of was hard work. Growing up, the only excess was the number of mouths to feed.

I don't know how Tracie managed it but she packed my things, booked my flight, and made sure I got to the airport on time. In my seat, I shut the partition door, closing myself off from the other passengers. Lowering my window shade, I pulled a sleep mask over my eyes. I just wanted the seventeen hours to pass as quickly as possible.

I think I was six or seven when I realized my dad wasn't like other dads. My father was flanked by security and was dressed in impeccably tailored suits. He was always coming from an important meeting or heading to one. I remember the way people would treat him, especially other men. They would hang on his every word and laugh at his jokes even when they weren't particularly funny. When my father entered a room, people moved out of his way.

I asked my mother once, "Is Daddy the president?" Because the President of the United States was the only person my young mind could conjure up who wielded that type of power. My mother reassured me that while we weren't a part of a political dynasty, my father was very powerful. Grover Thornton was the majority owner of a basketball team, the Las Vegas Ramblers.

My brother Benjamin and I were his children, but I think the Ramblers were his pride and joy. In the hierarchy of my father's attention, it was the Ramblers, Benji, my mother, then me. My father had no use for me. He didn't know how to connect with a little girl, a teenager, or an adult woman he couldn't sleep with. At least with Benji they could bond over sports or he could show him how to shave the scruffy whiskers on his chin.

With me, all I got were questions about school. And when I started dating, it was all about the importance of remaining a virgin. Then I went off to college and I think he was relieved he would no longer have to engage in those awkward conversations with me.

When the plane finally touched down in Las Vegas, I was exhausted. My attempts at sleep were frequently interrupted by intrusive thoughts. I just needed to lay eyes on my father. If I was able to see him, I'd know everything would be okay. When it was safe to do so, I took my phone off airplane mode. There were no new text messages from my mother or aunt, so I took that as a good sign. I texted Tracie letting her know I'd landed safely and thanked her for booking the flights and finishing up our trip alone.

Collecting my bag from baggage claim, I headed outside and easily spotted Charles, a tall and bulbous man in his fifties. He was leaning against a Mercedes Benz Maybach, one of my father's many cars.

"Hello Charles, good to see you again."

"You too, Miss Sariah. I hate that it has to be because of this." He opened the door and I slid inside. I waited as he placed my luggage in the trunk. Charles had been employed by my father since I was in junior high school. He was like an uncle to me even though my father didn't like us getting too familiar with the staff.

Charles climbed into the driver's seat and we were off. Normally he was a chatterbox, wanting to give me updates on his kids or listen to me chat about my travels. But today he was silent. The soft sounds of jazz could be heard through the speakers. I leaned back into my seat, watching the lights from the Vegas strip as we cruised down the freeway. My eyelids felt like weights were attached to them and before long, I drifted to sleep.

I was awakened by the sound of the driver door

opening and closing. Rubbing the sleep from my eyes, I peered out the window. Charles removed my bags from the trunk before opening my door.

"What are we doing at my mother's house? I thought you were taking me straight to the hospital?"

"Ms. Thornton asked that I bring you to her home," was the only explanation Mr. Charles offered. I followed him into the house and could distinctly hear a hum of conversation in the family room. "I'll take your bags upstairs." Charles ascended the steps, bags in hand, leaving me alone in the foyer. I walked toward the sound of voices. In the family room were my mother, my aunt, and a handful of other relatives.

"Sariah, your home," my Aunt Dina said when she caught sight of me.

My mother crossed the room, walking toward me. She looked like I felt … frazzled and depleted. I guess we were all operating under little sleep. My mother pulled me into a hug and her familiar scent provided temporary comfort. "I'm so sorry, Sariah," she said. "Your father is dead."

JUSTUS

I'M NOT GOING TO LIE, WHEN I GOT THE CALL THAT Grover Thornton was dead, my first thought was *What does this mean for the Ramblers' organization?* He'd been the owner for well over thirty years. I'm sure there was a succession plan in place, but his only living son was seven years old. And his daughter, Sariah, seemed more interested in travel and leisure than running a sports franchise.

This was a bad time to die. Not that it's ever convenient, but the Ramblers' organization needed structure and consistency, and Thornton's death would most likely shake up the team and put my players on edge. I'd been the head coach of the Ramblers for three years. The team was in a rebuilding phase and we were working hard to become playoff contenders. That meant two a day practices, team playbook training classes, and coddling the fragile egos of men who were earning millions of dollars to dribble a ball.

Before the Ramblers I was assistant head coach for the Charlotte Talons, who had won several Championships, so I knew a thing or two about winning. The

Ramblers team I inherited was far from winners. With overpaid superstar players, veteran players who'd grown disgruntled or lazy, and kids fresh out of college who came in guns blazing ready to prove themselves.

Pulling into a parking spot at the massive Baptist church, I place the car in park. I think this could be considered a mega church. Many prominent Black celebrities, politicians, and power players called Summit Baptist Church their home. Grover Thornton's homecoming was considered an event. Like booking tickets for a trendy show, people were clamoring to fill the pews.

Inside the church, I looked for a familiar face. The place was packed with rumbling from various conversations rolling through the building. I heard a sharp whistle and turned my attention to Deion "Deck" McCabe, the power forward for the Ramblers.

"Coach, over here," he shouted, despite the occasion being a somber event.

I shook my head because only Deck would do something like that. That man did not care what others thought of him, which I admired. At the pew, I greeted Deck and his girlfriend Sloane.

"Not you being on time," I teased, exchanging daps.

"I was not going to be late to the old man's funeral. Because you'd never let me hear the end of it."

The couple slid down, making room for me. I leaned forward, addressing Sloane. "How have you been?"

"Better than Grover Thornton," she said before flipping through the program. I overheard her whisper to Deck, "Jennifer Hudson is going to perform."

It was no secret Grover Thornton wasn't well liked. He was rich and powerful … respected even. But anyone who stepped up to that podium and said Thornton was a good man would be lying. He was a bully and an asshole. His business acumen was to be admired. Have others tell it he was great in the boardroom but he didn't bring that same type of dedication to his personal life. He had one failed marriage and another that was on the brink of collapse. And he rarely saw his children because he was always traveling.

My gaze fluttered around the room looking for anyone noteworthy. I spotted Rosaline Everly standing several pews ahead of me. She was an old Motown singer and a living legend. If this wasn't a funeral, I would have asked for her autograph for my father. He loved Motown, and I knew every Rosaline song by heart because he wore those albums out when I was a kid. *Baby don't break my heart. It's tearing me apart. How I love you so, you will never truly know. Say you love me, please say you love me.* I don't know what types of dudes Rosaline was messing with in her youth, but those men stayed doing her dirty. Which made for some amazing love songs.

My line of sight pushed past Ms. Everly to the front of the church. A statuesque woman in a purple dress was greeting attendees. Instinctually my eyes tripped down the length of her body, settling on her ass. It was perfectly rounded and poked out. That was an ass that pushed shit off the table when she passed by. After spending far too much time admiring her posterior, I moved on to her face. She was stunning. Her skin was the perfect shade of brown, deep and rich and glowing. Her hair cascaded over her shoulders. I don't know if it was real or fake, but it certainly didn't look cheap.

She had a face that implored you to fuck her in missionary because that way you gained access to her beautiful visage. Shaking my head, I tried to rattle the sexual thoughts loose. *You are in the house of God, have some respect.* I was taught God knew what you were thinking kind of like Santa Claus. But whenever I was in a church, I always felt like the building acted like Wi-Fi giving the Lord perfect reception to easily access my thoughts.

Right now my thoughts were far from sanctified. I quickly recited some Rosaline Everly to reset my brain. *Loving you is a lonely task. Why won't you love me back? I live for you, I breathe for you. You're all I want I can't sleep, can barely eat I'm like a fiend.* Damn Rosaline was down bad.

I hated funerals. I don't think anyone loved funerals, that would be macabre. But this particular funeral resembled a concert with big named R&B and soul artists returning to their religious roots with hymns about finding peace and walking hand and hand with God. I don't know if Grover Thornton was seeing the gates of heaven, but it was a nice sentiment. After the Clark Sisters made my eyes misty with their melodic tone, the lady in purple stepped up to the podium.

"My father had a saying 'If you're not willing to risk the usual, you will have to settle for the ordinary.'"

There were some murmurs in the audience, no doubt

from people who'd heard Grover say those words before … including me.

"My father was anything but ordinary. He was an immigrant moving to the states from Jamaica when he was ten. He quickly learned being broke was not a condition he wanted to endure forever. He took odd jobs, selling newspapers, mowing lawns, shining shoes. He was the first in his family to attend college graduating top of his class. My father was the definition of a hustler working hard to create the life he wanted. That was another Thornton saying 'Jelly Bean, create the life you want and you'll never be unhappy a day in your life.' My father did just that even when I didn't always understand it or appreciate it."

She stepped down and reclaimed her seat. Her speech was short and sweet and I got the sense she was encouraged to speak up more than having a burning desire to wax poetic about her old man. I also noticed what was missing. No sweet memories from childhood. No statements like "My father was …" insert positive attribute. Rumor has it that she and her father weren't very close and as a father of two daughters, I wondered how Thornton allowed that to happen.

After the funeral, I headed to Thornton's home for the repast. In all honesty, I wanted to skip the repast and go back to my place and pass out. But management made it clear they wanted a full showing at both the funeral and repast. As the coach, it would be a bad look to insist my players attend and then ghost the event.

The Thornton estate was massive. From the looks of the place, the Thorntons preferred a minimalist, monochromatic-design aesthetic that read cold and sterile. It felt like the place was for show and not for living. There were no family pictures on the wall and no sign of a child's toy. Everything was in its designated space. Thornton was probably just as demanding at home as he was at the office. If Grover visited my home, I imagine he would not have approved. Art work on the refrigerator, volleyball equipment in the entryway, and hair scrunchies and headbands hidden in plain sight in every room. The worse offense would most definitely be the family portraits on the wall. How dare I display family affection in full view for everyone to see?

The home was a hub of activity and although there had to be close to five hundred people, it didn't feel like it because the property was so large. Waiters in crisp, white shirts and black ties worked the room with appetizers. No deviled eggs, mac and cheese, and hot wings at this event. Which sucked because I was looking forward to a cocktail wiener covered in barbeque sauce.

Rubbing my sore left knee, I once again scanned the space and noted the sparce seating. When I woke up this morning my knees were tight and throbbing. Cold therapy and stretches helped to alleviate the pain, but I knew my limits. I would find the late Ms. Thornton, pay my respects, and stay for an hour tops. At the bar I ordered a seltzer water. It was far too early and the company was way too mixed for me to be tossing anything back.

A strong hand rapped me on my shoulders. "Hey Coach, how long do you think we need to be at this thing?" Deck asked.

"It's like you're reading my mind."

"Shit half these motherfuckers didn't even fuck with Thornton like that." Deck ordered vodka and coke and I shot him a warning eye. "On second thought just give me a ginger ale."

He did not need alcohol. Deck possessed the type of personality that was mellow until he wasn't and alcohol and Deck often turned out badly. At least it did when we were teammates. It had been a few years since we played together and we'd both grown since then, but I didn't want to take no damn chances. If one of these players so much as sneezed in the direction of the wrong person, I wouldn't hear the end of it.

Deck leaned close and whispered. "Did you peep the daughter's parting words for her pops?"

"Yeah, it seemed a little cold."

"Down right chilly if you ask me." He choked out a laugh. "Thornton was clearly the type that only a mother could love."

"Listen, if I had that man as a father, I think it would be difficult finding the fucks to give."

"What do you think happens to the Ramblers?"

"Hell if I know." I had tons of theories, but none I was willing to share with Deck. I'd learned early in my career if you tell a player something, the entire team would know within the hour.

Deck ribbed me in the side. "You know Thornton's wife is a free agent. Maybe it's the right time to swoop in and snag her."

"Not my type."

"Don't like sloppy seconds?"

"I like my money in my savings account. Not being swiped at Gucci and Louis Vuitton."

Tagging Deck in the arm, I walked away deciding to work the room by talking with some of the players and Ramblers staff. I passed by Patti Labelle and she smiled at me before I was pulled into a conversation about the Ramblers prospects for this season. I gave the only response I could, "We have a strong team. If we can avoid injuries and remain focused this could be a rewarding year."

Do you see what I just did there? I doled out a bunch of platitudes while promising nothing. After locating the widow in the backyard and offering words of condolence, I felt like my work here was done. It was almost three, if I left now, I could be home in sweats and watching TV by four. I made my way to the front door and out of the house with only two interruptions. When I hit the curb, I released a sigh.

"Are you sneaking out of my father's repast? You'll miss out on the spinach flatbread," Sariah Thornton called from behind me.

"Umm. No, I was just going for a walk." I thought it best to lie rather than tell a grieving daughter her father's funeral after party was mid.

She chuckled. "I know what that's code for. I'm down."

"To?" My eyebrow crept up my forehead.

"To go for a walk." Sariah hooked her arm in mine, leading me away from the house and up the block. She stopped at a small, deserted park tucked away in this palatial gated community. We sat at a picnic table and she drummed her fingernails on the metal surface expectantly.

I should be offended by her assumption I had a stash of the wacky tobaccy. But her belief was spot on, so I retrieved the vape pen from my breast pocket.

"What's it called?" she asked.

"Purple Urkel, it was created by the dude that played Steve Urkel on Family Matters."

She nodded. "I'm intrigued."

I handed her the pen, letting her take the first hit. She wrapped her lips around the tip and inhaled. When she exhaled, smoke wafted from her mouth and nose like a pro.

"My name's Sariah by the way." She handed the pen back to me.

"Justus." I took a hit. "I'm sorry about your father."

"Hmm … thank you."

"Losing a parent can be hard. I lost my mom when I was twelve."

"How'd she die?" Sariah asked, her words followed by circles of smoke.

"Childbirth."

"That sounds much worse than losing a parent when you're thirty-eight … like me."

"Doesn't really matter how old you are. Losing a parent sucks. If I lost my dad right now I wouldn't be able to function."

She eyed me but didn't utter a word.

"I didn't mean you should be curled up in the fetal position right now."

"Luckily for me my, father and I weren't very close."

"Sounds rather unfortunate and regrettable but what do I know?" I took another long drag feeling the weed work as intended, taking the edge off and smoothing me out.

"How did you know my father?"

"I'm the coach for the Ramblers."

"Coach Chappel?" Her mink eyes sparked with recognition.

"Yeah?"

"He spoke highly of you." She arched a perfect eyebrow and leaned close. "Does he know you're a pothead?" she teased.

"No, I don't think he did."

The playful smile faded from her face. "When a loved one passes, shouldn't you feel something?"

"Like what?"

"I don't know anger, sadness, relief even. I feel nothing."

"Everyone is different. Sometimes it can take months for shit to really sink in."

Her eyes glazed over and she focused on some point off in the distance. "I just want this celebration of life to end so I can get back to mine." She gasped and turned to me. "That was really horrible of me to say so I'd appreciate it if you didn't repeat it."

"No judgment and no snitching. What happens in the park in a gated community for the rich and richer stays there," I assured her.

We took several more hits of the vape pen in silence before an older woman approached us. "Sariah what the hell are you doing?"

The smoke I was attempting to push from my lungs got lodged in my throat while I fumbled to hide the vape pen. I felt like a high school sophomore getting caught on the bleachers by the math teacher.

"Nothing Aunt Dina, I was just talking to Coach Chappel." Sariah stood and shimmied a little to adjust her dress.

"There is a crowd of people wanting to extend their condolences."

"I'm sure there is," she hissed.

Aunt Dina's head craned left and right trying to process what we were up to. "Have you two been smoking that reefer?"

"No Auntie. We were just talking. And now you're embarrassing me." Lucky for Sariah the Purple Urkel had a pleasant grape scent, so no one had to be the wiser.

"Come on, let's head back to the house." Aunt Dina's tone was harsher then it needed to be on a day like this.

Sariah followed behind her auntie. Turning briefly, she mouthed the words "Sorry."

SARIAH

I woke up in the guest room of my mother's house. It was still dark outside, but I couldn't sleep. Today the family would head to the lawyer's office for the reading of the will. After this last obligation I could return home to New York and move past this. My mother had been smothering me this entire week. She wanted to make sure I was okay. But when I told her I was fine, she didn't believe me.

She was right to be concerned. What kind of person is fine after they lose a parent so unexpectedly? I was never big on showing my emotions. Especially the ones that made me most vulnerable like love or sadness. Everyone was looking at me with a watchful eye, waiting for my visage to crack and for me to dissolve into tears. Crying was the last thing I was worried about. When I thought about my father, the only emotion I could easily access was anger.

I decided to get up and go for a run, hoping it would help to settle the thoughts tumbling around in my brain. Popping in my ear buds, I selected a hip-hop playlist that always got me amped up when I needed motivation. First up was a techno rap song by XYZ Baby called I Thought You Knew. Techno wasn't usually my vibe, but the bass in the song and the timbre in his voice just did something to me.

As my feet bounced against the pavement, I was tempted to stop for a quick dance break. Which of course I didn't do, because I was in mourning. The last thing I needed were nosy neighbors claiming I was overjoyed at the loss of our patriarch. Being the daughter of Grover Thornton came with attention. Mostly unwanted. It was great when I had a new product to push but not so much when I was exiting a nightclub with a mystery man.

If I turned my brain on low it was as if nothing had changed. A normal visit to Vegas like I did every few months or so to appease my mother. After my run we'd have breakfast and maybe play tennis at Sand Springs Country Club. Members would stop by our table for a quick chat or a bit of gossip. Women who my mother had known for years would ask about my dad. I'd say he was fine. Because on this very normal day my father wasn't dead, he was just away on business. Maybe he was in California, Spain, or Dubai.

Coach Chappel mentioned it could take months for me to fully comprehend the loss of my father. Would I be in the freezer section at Whole Foods picking out frozen fruit for my smoothies and dissolve into uncontrollable tears because it finally dawned on me my father was never coming back?

After running three miles one way, I opted to walk home. My watch chimed, notifying me of an incoming call. I accepted and the call interrupted my playlist. "Hello?"

"Hey you're up?" Tracie asked.

"Yeah, I went for a run. You're still coming today, right?" I'd asked Tracie to accompany me to the reading of the will. Not so much for the will part but for the possibility of grabbing drinks afterward.

"Yep, I'll be at your mom's place by nine." Knowing her she'd be here much earlier, she was never late and liked to give herself a fifteen-minute cushion.

"I was thinking we should start looking for flights back home," I said, wiping sweat from my eyes.

"Are you sure? You don't want to hang out with your mother for a bit longer? There's no rush Sariah, you should take all the time you need."

"I'm not rushing. I'm just ready to sleep in my own bed."

"Alright we can talk more about it later on today." I knew that meant she would attempt to change my mind and encourage me to focus on myself. Which I couldn't do even if I wanted to. We had a launch coming up and while it was still months away, every step was meticulously planned. If we missed one deadline it would cause a chain reaction.

"There's nothing to talk about because it's settled."

"You don't need to make any rash decisions."

"This isn't rash. I've thought about it. In fact it's all I've thought about. Jumping back into work is just what I need."

Tracie released a long sigh, adding her dissenting opinion on record without uttering a single word.

"I'll see you in a few." I ended the call. This topic was not up for debate.

If I had my way, we would go from the lawyer's office to the airport and be back in New York by midnight. I didn't want to remain in Vegas any longer than I had to. This place was no longer my home. It stopped feeling like a home long before my father's death. This was why I always urged my mother to come visit me.

It was New York. We could shop, take in a show, and eat at the best restaurants. Most of the time that pitch worked, but occasionally my mother would guilt me into making the trip out west not just for her, but to touch bases with family who asked her about me frequently. The last time I was here, my dad and I got into a verbal slug match. We never saw eye to eye and at that point, I think we were both actively looking for things to criticize one another on. Not going to lie, knowing my last words to my father were "I can't stand to be in the same room with you" sucked.

The law offices of Feinberg, Smit, and Kramer were on the top floor of an all-glass building. My mother, Aunt Dina, Tracie, and I filed into a conference room already occupied by Harper, my father's second wife and her lawyer. Exchanging pleasantries, we took our seats.

"Looks like we're ready to get started. It's so good to see you again Colette." Archie Smit greeted my mother.

"Thank you, Archie."

"Well I'm not going to keep you waiting. How this works is I'll read from Grover's last will and testament word for word. After the reading if you have any questions, please feel free to ask them or if you prefer, we can schedule a private meeting." Mr. Smit pulled out a small stack of papers approximately ten pages long. "I Grover Thornton being of sound mind and body ..."

I barely listened as he ran through the formal legalize but my ears perked up when Mr. Smit mentioned my mother.

"To my beloved ex-wife Colette Thornton I leave twenty million dollars and the house in the Hamptons."

I snuck a glance at my mother. She loved that twelve-bedroom home with private beach front access. Her face was like a marble statue but I knew on the inside she was beaming. When she and my father divorced, my mother was heartbroken she didn't get the home. During the divorce she walked away with almost half of my father's fortune since she'd been with my dad well before he amassed his vast wealth. As the ex-wife, the fact she was included in the will was surprising.

"To my wife Harper Thornton and pursuant to our executed prenuptial agreement I leave one hundred million dollars, the home in Las Vegas and the home in Aspen. For my son Zander Thornton a trust has been established with fifty million dollars and various stocks and bonds." Harper's eyes pinged across the room as she calculated the money she and her son were inheriting and the cash and assets that still remained.

"To my daughter and first born, Sariah Thornton I leave the remainder of my wealth. All other residential and commercial properties including but not limited to New York, London, Colorado, and the island in Bali. I also bequeath majority ownership of the Las Vegas Ramblers to Sariah Thornton along with all other business ventures, the Thornton winery in Napa, the Premier Travel Jets, and the hotels and entertainment assets. My car collection will be split equally between my two children …"

Mr. Smit kept talking but I was having difficulty processing the information. My father was leaving me damn near everything he owned. Why the fuck would he do this?

"That concludes the reading of Mr. Thornton's will. Are there any questions?"

The tension in the room was palpable and most of it was coming from Harper's direction. It was evident from the incredulous expression on her face she believed she and her son deserved a bigger portion of the assets. "Is that it?" Harper asked.

"Yes, that is all," Mr. Smit said.

"Are you sure?" Harper continued.

"I am quite certain."

"Do we get copies of this document? How do we even know this was Grover's final wishes? I'm having a hard time—"

"I have a question," I chimed in. "When was his will last updated?"

"We reviewed your father's will annually to make sure there were no changes. His last annual review was …" Mr. Smit flipped through some papers. "Seven months ago."

A heaviness settled in my chest. "I need to go. I need fresh air." Standing I collected my things.

"Baby, are you alright?" my mother asked.

"No, I am not alright," I screeched far too loudly, based on my mother's displeased expression. "I'm sorry. I just need to go. I'll meet you back at the house."

Tracie followed me to the elevator. When we were safely inside, she said. "Oh my fucking God."

WE ORDERED A RIDEX AND HEADED TO A HOLE IN THE wall bar off the strip. This was the kind of place for people who needed a taste first thing in the morning. It was noon, but I ordered a Moscow Mule.

"I let you contemplate shit on the ride over here but the suspense is killing me. What are you thinking?"

"I didn't think he was going to leave me out of the will ..."

Tracie raised a brow and tilted her head, silently calling bullshit.

"Okay, maybe I thought there was a slim chance he would exclude me."

"But he didn't. He left you the lion's share. You own a winery now."

I dropped my face into my hands. "It's too much."

"It's what he thought you deserved."

"What I deserved was a present father figure. Who actually came to important events instead of sending flowers."

"Maybe this is his way of making up for that. His way of saying, 'I'm sorry I missed much of your childhood, here is a private island in Bali to smooth things over.'"

My nerves were raw and I was on the verge of throwing an expletive-filled temper tantrum. "I just want to go home."

"And now you can, in one of the jets in your fleet of private airplanes."

"Why did he give me the basketball team? The winery, the jets, the hotels I get that ... sort of. But the Ramblers?"

"You said it's always been his baby so I guess he wanted to ensure it was in good hands."

"If that was the case, he wouldn't have given it to me. I don't know anything about running a basketball team. I know even less about basketball."

"Sariah, you run a successful business."

"Beauty and basketball aren't the same. Not even close."

"Sure there will be some differences but at the core it's all very similar."

I stretched my face in disbelief. "Why would he do this? Was this one final fuck you on the way out the door?"

"Your father leaves you billions of dollars and you think there's some type of catch?"

"Yeah, to have me fail miserably and be the final reminder the wrong child survived."

Tracie's expression switched from jovial to serious. "Don't go there. He never thought that."

"He did. And it's fine." I tossed back the rest of my drink, flagging the bartender to request another.

"What are you going to do?"

"I'm going to go home. I don't want any of this. Can you decline an inheritance?"

"I think you need to give this time. Don't make any decisions you'll regret later. Just let everything marinate for a bit. Maybe you should consult someone in the Ramblers' organization. Someone you can trust. Pick their brain. You don't even know what all goes into being the majority owner of a basketball team."

"You make it sound like my father left me a small farm with chickens and a cow named Masie. That I could handle."

"I would love to see you stomping around a farm milking cows and collecting eggs."

"Old Sariah had a farm," I sang, causing us both to descend into a much-needed fit of laughter.

Back at my mother's house, I listened as she tried to convince me this was a blessing and I deserved the world and this was my father's way of giving it to me.

"Maybe you're right," I finally offered, knowing she didn't want to listen to me whine about inheriting a fortune.

She flashed her bright smile before saying, "Oh I almost forgot." My mother walked over to the kitchen island and grabbed an envelope from the counter. Returning to the breakfast nook, she handed the envelope to me. "You left so quickly that Archie didn't have time to give you this."

The envelope had my name on it. "What is it?"

"It's a letter from your father."

I flipped the envelope over in my hands.

"Well, aren't you going to open it?"

"I … I'm tired and I have a headache. I just kind of want to go to bed."

She pulled her face, wearing a disappointed expression. "Okay dear. You get some rest. Do you want me to make you some tea to take up?"

"Yeah, that would actually be really nice."

My mother placed extra tea in an insulated thermos, so I was now enjoying a second cup after a quick shower, cozied up in bed. I looked to the note I'd tossed on the bedside table. The last thing I wanted to do right now was read my father's final words to me. Money was not an issue for me. Genuine Beauty was doing well and making millions. So my father could have left me with nothing and I would have been good.

Instead he did the exact opposite, leaving me with so much that I lost track of all the assets. At the time of his death his projected net worth was just under ten billion. Maybe if my father had just left me cash, I'd be less vexed. The vast source of his wealth came from investments, real estate, and business ventures. Those type of assets needed to be managed. I certainly didn't have the bandwidth to oversee them all. My father left me these properties to do with as I saw fit, but I knew liquidating my newly acquired assets would have him rolling in his grave. But maybe that's what he deserved … for everything he worked so hard for, at the expense of spending time with his kids, to be sold off bit by bit to the highest bidder.

It wasn't my responsibility to carry on his legacy. I had my own destiny to solidify. And if that was something he wanted, he should have told me. Laying his kingdom at my feet with no directions, no support and no guardrails was careless of him. Normally a parent would work closely with their children, teaching them all about the family business so in the event of their untimely death, the wheels could keep spinning.

Giving me the world with no education on how to navigate it was selfish. And I would not be burdened with his last wishes. What about what I wanted? I bet he never paused for one second to ask himself what was best for Sariah. Even in death, all he cared about was himself.

JUSTUS

WORD SPREAD QUICKLY ABOUT SARIAH THORNTON'S inheritance of the Ramblers. I'll admit I did not see Grover Thornton handing the keys to his empire to his daughter. In my three years with the team, I'd never seen her attend a game. But now that the news was public, I was working overtime assuaging the fears of the players. Any time there was a change in ownership it was expected that questions about the future of the team would follow. Grover had a vision for the Ramblers. In that vision, I played a prominent role. I had zero assurances Sariah Thornton carried that same vision.

Joining the growing crowd, I headed down to the meeting room where the entire organization was gathered. Sariah Thornton would be addressing us all as a group and I was hopeful her speech would provide clarity. It had been two weeks since the announcement of new ownership and since then, I'd been inundated by an endless barrage of rumors at work and unsubstantiated news reports in the media.

"Is that Montell from the cafeteria?" Deck asked

from the seat next to me. Damn everyone is in this bitch. But according to Coach there's nothing to worry about."

"Because there's not. She isn't going to come in here swinging a big stick and breaking shit."

"I heard that she hated her father and she plans to destroy the team before selling it," Colin Pratt whispered on the opposite side of me.

"Now why would she do that? That's not a smart investment."

"Because she's already rich and she knows her pops was dedicated to this team so she wants to crumble his empire," Colin continued.

"Where did you hear that?" Deck asked.

"TMZ," Colin said with a serious face.

"See this is exactly why I can't trust anything you fools say," I said.

"Well I heard something different," Deck said. "The part about her hating her father, that's true but she's looking to clean house. She wants to build this team on her own from the bottom up. So when the Ramblers start winning she doesn't have to share any of the success with her old man. She can claim she did it all on her own." Deck split an orange offering me half.

I popped a wedge in my mouth. This was my biggest fear. I'm sure just like Colin's intel the source wasn't reliable but Sariah wanting to put her mark on the organization was very likely. That would bode poorly for me and my coaching staff. In most transfers of ownership, the coaching team was the first to go. Owners wanted to bring in people they trusted and hand selected. Sariah didn't know me from a can of paint, so she had no reason to keep me or the staff on if she was considering a change.

As always, the players were looking to me for their cues. If I freaked out, they would follow suit. My confidence in the team and organization could not waiver publicly. I had to pretend it was business as usual. Players could sense fear, that's how they dominated other teams. So my demeanor needed to remain fearless and unbothered or shit would spiral out of control quickly. And once the players' trust in this institution was gone, it would be damn near impossible to reel them back in.

"Listen, in a few minutes we're going to hear her tell us exactly what she's thinking so let's cool it with the predictions and conjecture."

"You're not even the least bit concerned?" Colin asked. This response was out of character for him because he oozed confidence. Which was partially deserved, he was the Ramblers' star player. But in my opinion his star didn't shine nearly as bright as it did several years ago.

"No." There was a finality to my tone. Letting the two men know I was done talking about this.

The small auditorium was standing room only. Everyone in the organization wanted to be present to see the new owner with their own eyes. When I say everyone was here, I meant it. The players, coaching staff, the medical team, the trainers. As Deck noted, even some of the cafeteria crew was in attendance. Sariah's next move could impact all of us.

When she entered the room, the loud conversations

subdued to a soft rumble. Walking to the middle of the stage, Sariah pulled the microphone from the podium. She looked just as beautiful as she did the last time I'd seen her. On this occasion, however, she was rocking a more upbeat color. The blush-toned, wide-leg pants and silk blouse complimenting her glowing brown skin.

Raising the microphone to her lips, she recoiled when ringing audio feedback filled the air. Sariah shot a glance at some unknown face in the audience. A look that said fix this shit or you'll be escorted from the building by security. It was subtle, but I could make out a distinct fierceness in her big brown eyes.

The microphone grew silent. "Now that I have your attention ..." Her indifferent expression could not conceal the shaky tone of her voice. "Thank you for taking time out from your busy schedules to be here." She looked out into the capacity crowd and it was like a switch was turned on. Maybe she realized a mild delivery would be lost on this group. Her back straightened conveying confidence. Clearly this wasn't her first time in front of an audience and she was completely in command of the room.

When she spoke again, her voice was as clear as a bell. "So I know many of you have heard the rumors and I wanted to come here and address a few. Yes, I am the new owner of the Ramblers. Yes, I understand my father's shoes were enormous and will be difficult to fill. Yes, at this time I intend to remain the majority owner of the organization."

You could hear a pin drop and from the faces of the players and staff, no one knew how to react.

"As such I'm looking forward to getting to know each and every one of you better. I'm in Vegas for the full week and I hope to meet with the executive managers and the head and assistant coaches. In the coming weeks I will be scheduling individual meetings with the players and small group meetings with the remaining staff. I want to add that no one is getting fired. At least not yet."

Sariah set the mic down before reclaiming it to add. "I've heard that the goal of an NBA team is to win games. Something that the Ramblers seem to be lacking. If you do not further the goal of winning us games, your time with this organization may soon come to a close. Thank you." She returned the microphone to the podium stand and exited the room not hanging around for questions.

Well that was hella ominous. She essentially said no one is getting fired but your ass may get fired. Hearing she intended to meet with the staff was welcomed news. I think it's important to get to know your team before making any sweeping changes. Far too often new management came in with something to prove, so they implemented these big changes to demonstrate their power before fully understanding the nature of the business or the culture embedded within it. I was happy to see Sariah wasn't one of those leaders.

My intention was to return to my office and finish up some outstanding items while I waited for my meeting with the new owner. Unfortunately, little to no work was accomplished because my staff and players kept interrupting me. It appeared all anyone could talk about was Sariah Thornton. Why they all felt the need to pick my brain, I didn't know. I was working with the same information they were and I wasn't interested in what ifs.

A little before three, I made my way to the executive suites which were located on the other side of the Ramblers campus. It was a short walk from the training center, but it might as well have been in a whole other zip code because the atmosphere at both buildings was night and day.

At the seventy thousand square-foot training facility, the vibe was laid back. Everyone was friendly and greeted you when you walked by. Yes, I was chewing out the team daily, but we left that shit on the court. Throughout the halls, gym, and cafeteria, it was all love. In comparison, the executive building was cold and sterile. And I got the sense I was always being watched. There were no boisterous conversations or laughter sprinkling out of offices. In fact, all the executives kept their doors closed. Don't even think about stopping by to chat. If you didn't have an appointment, which oftentimes had to be scheduled weeks in advance, you weren't allowed in.

In the lobby, guests were required to show their badge and sign in at the front desk. Once it was confirmed you in fact had a reason for entering the holy sanctum, you were granted access to a bank of elevators that took you to a specific floor. I called it purgatory because it was a floor designed to contain visitors. From there an assistant would escort you the remainder of the way.

After jumping through all the hoops, I was allowed entry to Grover Thornton's office, which was now Sariah Thorton's office, for our one-on-one meeting.

Klay, my assistant coach, was leaving his meeting with a bewildered expression on his face.

"Hey, how'd it go?" I asked.

Klay walked over and whispered, "I can't read her. I don't know if she liked what I said or hated it. She just nodded and took occasional notes. He scrubbed his face with his hands. "I did tell her how great you were and how much I liked working under you," he half teased.

"Thanks I'll pay you later."

"Coach Chappel, Ms. Thornton will see you now," Grover's longtime executive assistant announced, waving me over.

"Good luck Coach," Klay said with a pat to my shoulder. He followed the same assistant who'd escorted me up back the way we'd came.

Sariah stood when I entered the office, extending her hand when I covered the distance between us. Her hand was soft and touching her made my face flush.

"Good to see you again," I said.

"Have we met before?" She raised an eyebrow.

"Is that your way of saying I didn't make a strong impression?"

"No … you made an impression."

"I just want to mention that weed is legal in the state of Nevada."

"If I were looking to fire you it wouldn't be over the weed smoking. Are you going to give me back my hand?"

I was still vigorously shaking her appendage. "Sorry about that." I released my claim.

She led me to a seating nook in the corner of the room with amazing views of the Las Vegas strip. Even in the light of day the skyline was impressive.

"So I'm asking everyone three questions."

"No small talk first?" I joked, hoping to settle my growing nerves.

"I hate small talk. Plus I've conducted several interviews today and my social battery is almost depleted."

"I agree small talk is the worst. Sometimes the silence doesn't need to be filled with observations of the unusually cool weather."

"It *has* been unusually cool for this time of year."

"I wore a jacket this weekend."

"It's not cold enough for a jacket."

"It was Saturday night and it was damn near nippy."

"That's a word you don't hear every day," Sariah noted.

"It's my mission to bring some of the old school phrases and words back."

"Old school phrases?"

"Yeah, the stuff our parents used to say. Things like 'Don't take any wooden nickels.'"

"That is definitely a lost phrase because I've never heard it."

"Well now you have and you can just throw it into any conversation to keep it in the lexicon."

"I think that's a mission that is solely your own."

Klay was wrong, she wasn't hard to read. The glint in her eye let me know I had her attention and the way her body was positioned, with her long legs crossed in my direction, indicated she felt at ease in my presence. As an athlete your job was to anticipate what your opponent was going to do before they did it. I had a PHD in body language.

"Question one. What do you love most about this organization?"

Taking a deep breath, I shifted into professional mode. "That's easy. I've worked for a lot of teams as a player and coach and one thing that is hard to find is the family atmosphere. I'm talking about the coaching staff and players, the doctors and medical professionals, food service and custodians. I enjoy coming to work each day. I know it won't be easy and some days I have to pop several aspirins for my stress headache and Prilosec for my congealed gut, but it's all worth it. I'm sure that all probably sounds corny and cliche but it's true."

"It's not corny," she whispered. Her eyes settled on my face. Her gaze was intense like she was attempting to connect on a spiritual level. And I was down with that. Let's connect physically, spiritually, mentally, and orally. I'd take all of it.

"Question two: What do you dislike about the organization?"

"There's a lack of trust between executive management and the coaching staff. I don't have issues with healthy discourse but I was hired to do a job. So if I choose to bench a player or start McCabe instead of Perkins that should be my call. We all want the same thing."

"To win?"

"Yes, I make the choices I do with the information I have at the time in hopes that it leads to success. No one wants to win more than I do. But expectations need to meet reality."

"Are you saying that executive expectations don't meet the reality based on the players?"

"It's a process and the Ramblers are currently knee deep in the rebuilding phase. But some people are only interested in results. If you rush the rebuilding process, sure you may have some success but it won't be sustainable."

"Did you like my father?"

My head jerked back. "Is that really the third question you're asking people?"

"No, but it's the question I'm asking you."

This was a trick question. She was probably testing me to see if I was loyal. Fuck it, I wasn't going to lie.

"No one is perfect and while your father was a good businessman, I think he lacked some interpersonal skills."

Her eyebrow rose in a slow arch. I wasn't sure if I'd passed or failed her quiz. She stood, retrieving a glass of water before leaning against her desk. "What's the endgame for you Coach?"

"I thought I only had to answer three questions," I joked. One that did not elicit any amusement from her.

"I'm adding another one. When you're the boss you can do that."

I clipped my head into a nod. Standing, I crossed the room, stopping directly in front of her. "A championship. I've won several championships as a coach with other teams and I'm hoping to do the same here."

"Can we win with our current lineup?"

"I'm invested in this team but we need time, we need to make some trades, and we need fresh talent."

She tilted her head like she was weighing her options. "Thank you for your candor."

"You're welcome. I appreciate that you're taking the time to meet with the staff. It'll help make this change less scary."

"Am I scary?" She tugged at her jacket. "I specifically wore pink because of its non-scary aesthetic."

I stammered until I was able to recover my thoughts. "Uhm … well … no. Change is scary. You are the opposite of scary. You're delightful. Like a spot of tea." I don't know why I spoke that last sentence in a British accent.

"Thank you, Coach Chappel." I could tell she was suppressing a laugh.

Making my way to the door, I stopped short. "By the way how are you holding up?"

"With what?"

"The loss of your father."

"I'm fine." Her tone implied she thought I was stupid for asking a question like that. Of course she was fine, she'd just inherited a bazillion dollars.

"I didn't mean to pry."

"No … you're not prying. It just doesn't feel real. But I know it is because I had to get all dressed up today and pretend like I know what the fuck I'm doing when I haven't got a clue." She closed her eyes and breathed deep. "I hope that my confession of incompetence will stay in this room."

"Your secret is safe with me. And if it's any consolation you have this organization shaking in their boots. Scary isn't always a bad thing. When people feel threatened, they tend to straighten up and pay attention."

SARIAH

"I'M PRETTY SURE EVERYONE HATES ME."

"It couldn't have gone that bad," Tracie tried to reassure me via video chat.

"Everyone was staring, waiting for me to say something profound and ease their fears. And I wanted to tell them sorry guys we're all fucked."

"How did the interviews go?"

"Okay I guess."

"Did you identify a potential candidate for Operation Ramblers 101?"

"The GM is out. He was my father's right-hand man but I get the sense he lacks the patience required for this job."

"GM?"

"General Manager."

"Look at you and your sports lingo."

"Is that considered sports lingo?"

"I thought GM stood for gloss mattifier so yes you speak sports now," she said while scarfing down a poke bowl.

Tracie was a pro at spinning several plates at once.

Right now she was talking me through a crisis while eating a late dinner, enjoying a face mask, and checking her phone for the influx of emails. Emails I still needed to sort through. When did Genuine Beauty become my five to nine job after my nine to five? I agreed to cosplay as an NBA owner, but if it interfered with my ability to focus on my real job, I would pass the ball so fast heads would spin.

Flipping through the personnel files my new Ramblers executive assistant, Bethany, gathered for me, I stopped at Justus Chappel's hefty file. "The coach looks promising."

After brainstorming with Tracie I decided to hold off on selling while I learned all I could about the organization, team, and sport. To do that, we both agreed I needed a silent mentor who would show me the ropes while keeping my need for tutelage quiet.

"What do you like about him?"

What *didn't* I like about him? Justus was tall, clocking in at six feet, six inches. He was muscular but lean. His skin was a beautiful chestnut complexion, and it looked like he took care of it. Which led me to wonder what woman was performing self-care Sunday with him. He was handsome in an unassuming way but when he smiled, it all made sense. He also had a beard which was my kryptonite. There was just something about a man with a beard that gave grown and sexy.

At forty-four, Mr. Chappel was grown enough to know how to make a woman's toes curl.

I likened myself as the dick whisperer. With the ability to forecast what was between a man's legs from a mile away. It was mostly in their stride. The way Justus walked, confident but not cocky with a slight limp. And when he sat, he kept a wide girth, presumably so as not to crush the jewels.

"Hello? Did your connection freeze?"

"No, I'm still here." I dropped the file and refocused my attention on Tracie.

"So tell me what's the deal with the coach?"

Aside from the incredible qualities I'd run through in my head, Tracie was probably asking about tangible attributes. "Well I've had the opportunity to talk to him twice now. Once at the repast and then again today. Both times he seemed straightforward and honest. And he's easy to talk to."

"Do you think he'd keep your secret?"

"I do. He comes off as the type of man whose word is his bond. Plus he was the only person to ask how I was doing after …"

"So he's empathetic. Gold star for the coach. Any other possibles?"

"No."

"Well then Coach Chappel sounds like your man."

"Or I could just sell the team, cut my losses, and move on."

"We discussed this."

"I just feel like I'm delaying the inevitable. I have my own company to run. I can't expect you to pull all the weight. We have so much work to do in preparation for the skincare launch in a few months."

"Don't worry about me. I have your back just like you had mine when I went through my divorce. I was useless for like seven months and you kept the whole thing running while ensuring I was taken care of. You made me soup."

"I bought it."

"Bought, made, the same difference. I'm just saying you supported me and now it's time for me to return the favor."

Relief collapsed my shoulders. It was nice not having to put on a brave face all the time. Between my father's passing, the flood of calls from all the businesses and properties searching for answers, and the press hounding me about the Ramblers and my plan for the team, my plate was full. "I don't think I could navigate this mess without you."

"That's what friends are for." She brushed my words off. "Reach out to the coach and schedule a sit down. And call me after you two talk. I want to know what he said."

"Will do. Thanks again." Ending our call, I closed my laptop.

Coach Chappel was like my Obi-Wan Kenobi. He was my only hope. I was in over my head and feared everyone could tell I was floundering. The coach could act as my lifeline. Something I could tether myself to so I didn't veer too far off course. But how do I ask him to be my mentor? And what if he said no? I still had dozens of interviews to conduct, but I was certain Coach Chappel was the best choice. What I was asking for was discretion and an intense knowledge transfer. He knew the sport being a former player and now coach, but more importantly, he understood the organization. If I wanted to succeed, I needed to immerse myself in Ramblers culture.

Reaching for Justus's file, I located his phone number. I should just call him right now. If I gave myself time to think, I'd back out. The phone rang several times, so I was expecting it to go to voicemail.

"Hello?" He finally picked up.

"So you just answer your phone raw like that? You don't even screen your calls first. I could be a telemarketer," I said.

"I have two fourteen-year-old daughters so I always answer my phone. Who's this?"

"Oh sorry, I probably should've led with my name. It's Sariah. Sariah Thornton. From the Ramblers club … team … league." Shit, rookie mistake. I needed to Google basketball terms so I didn't sound like such a newbie.

"Good evening Ms. Thornton. How can I help you?" The ease in his voice stiffened as his tone took on a formal quality.

"I was hoping you were free for dinner on Wednesday. I had some follow-up questions I wanted to ask you."

"Umm … Wednesday can work if we make it a late dinner. My daughter is in a school play and when I'm in town I try not to miss my girls' events."

I did my best to ignore my heart melting. A man that showed up for his kids was a keeper. "Would nine give you enough time?"

"Nine would be perfect."

"Great."

"I look forward to seeing you again." I knew his statement was strictly platonic, but his words in conjunction with the rich timbre of his voice, sent a whoosh of heat up my neck and caused my lady parts to swell. "Have a good night."

Do you want to come over here and guarantee my night was a great one? Obviously, I didn't say that, opting instead for a curt, "You too." Ending the call, I sunk into my mattress. This was business only. But Justus being nineties sitcom fine complicated things. I had to remind myself this wasn't about fucking, this was about fixing the mess I was in. So that meant I needed to keep my legs closed and my mind open. Yes, he was my type and in any other situation I would have staked my claim and made my intentions very clear.

"Strictly business."

Now I just had to convince him to help me out of the kindness of his heart. Or I could threaten his job, but that seemed unethical, and like something my father would do. The last thing I wanted was to follow his "at any cost" ideology. He didn't care who he had to step over or push aside. And he definitely didn't care about showing up late to my birthday because a meeting ran long. I'd have to make Justus believe this was beneficial for the both of us. How I was going to do that, I wasn't quite sure.

SINCE I LIVED IN NEW YORK, I DIDN'T HAVE A HOME IN Vegas. The Waldorf Astoria offered condos on the top floors of their hotel. I signed a six-month lease for a two-bedroom luxury apartment with concierge and access to the hotel amenities. Which included the pool, spa, and room service from the five-star restaurants on the ground floor. Working with the concierge, I booked a nine o'clock dinner reservation at the steak house on site.

I made sure to arrive before Coach Chappel so I could have a drink to soothe my nerves. If you hadn't noticed by now, I wasn't a person who asked for help. One thing my father taught me was to be independent, seeing as I had to learn not to rely on him at a young age. If I could do it on my own, I usually did. When I couldn't, I hired someone to help me. It wasn't a favor when it came with compensation.

Sitting in the dimly lit restaurant, I regretted inviting Justus to meet me. I should have just enrolled in YouTube University. Everything I needed to know about being an owner was probably there. The way I kept fidgeting with my hair and outfit, anyone watching would think I was waiting for the arrival of a first date. I certainly fretted over what to wear in hopes of making a strong impression. Finally settling on a black sheath dress that showcased my arms, hugged my curves, and offered a little leg with a high slit. Simple gold jewelry and a strappy heeled sandal accentuated the look. My hair cascaded over my shoulders in large, fluffy curls. I wanted Coach Chappel to understand that while I was asking for help, I wasn't some damsel in distress.

When I caught sight of Justus heading toward my table, it threw my heart out of cadence. This man was fine. He was the type of brother women prayed for. Tall, well groomed, good natured, sexy as hell. If this wasn't a business dinner, I'd most definitely add his banana to my fruit salad. Justus was dressed in a suit, tailored with a blue and gold tie and accompanying pocket square that left me wet. I also noted his ring finger was bare. Which didn't mean he was single but left the door open to the possibility.

I stood as he approached.

"Hi," he said with a crooked grin.

"Hello." I leaned forward awkwardly. Should I shake his hand, hug him, or fuck him on the table?

"Are we hugging?" he asked cautiously.

"We can hug." My intent was to sound nonchalant. Coach Justus leaned in and respectfully placed his hand on the middle of my back. I wrapped a polite arm around him, drinking him in. He smelled divine. Like doughnuts and black licorice. Yes, it was a crazy combination, but it worked. And I knew immediately that being this close to his warm, hard body was a mistake.

He let me go, placing his hand on the top of my chair, encouraging me to sit. When I was seated, he unbuttoned his suit jacket and claimed the seat across from me. "I hope you weren't waiting too long?"

"No, I just got here."

"What are you drinking?"

"A Manhattan."

He wrinkled his nose at me. "Damn, you're kind of hardcore."

"Am I?"

"Whiskey puts hair on your chest. I'm a bit of a lightweight." When the waiter approached, he ordered a Tom Collins. "This place is nice. I don't think I've ever been here before."

"It has a cool vibe," I agreed, appreciating the ambiance with fresh eyes: the rich walnut wood tables and the high-backed velvet chairs. Hanging from the ceiling were large, circular glass fixtures and the illumination danced on the surface of our table, causing everything the light touched to sparkle.

"It would be good for a date night."

The butterflies in my stomach abruptly stopped. "Yeah, you should definitely bring your significant other for dinner or drinks. I'm sure they'd love it." Did you see what I just did there? Let's hope I get the right response.

"I will keep that in mind for my next Flirt Chat date."

The corners of my mouth pulled upward. I had to block my face with the menu until I could regain control over my exhilaration upon hearing of his unattached status.

"See anything that interests you?" he asked.

I lowered the menu giving him the once over. *Sariah this isn't a blind date. You need this man to work with you not work you over. But why couldn't it be both?* Yes, it was messy, but he was hard to resist and he wasn't even trying. "There's so many tempting options but I'm going to order the short ribs."

"That sounds good." He licked his lips. Lips I was plotting to feel pressed against mine.

"You should get it too."

"No … if you're getting the short ribs, I should order something totally different. That way we can share."

My eyes doubled in size. I knew this wasn't a date … but did he? Sharing plates was reserved for close friends and lovers. I wonder which category he was looking to land in. Or maybe he was just being nice because I was his new boss.

Clearing his throat, Justus continued, "We don't have to share it's fine."

"No, I think sharing is smart. We get to taste more of the menu."

"Exactly. So do you have any allergies or things you refuse to put in your mouth?"

News flash: I would put it so deep in my mouth I would have to breathe through my nose. "Peas are a no go but other than that dealer's choice."

He ordered a shrimp and pasta dish. This wasn't a date. But if it were, it would be going really well.

"So how was your daughter's play?"

"She was amazing. I may be a little biased." He had a habit of stroking his jaw with the back of his hand.

"What was the play about?"

"It was called See Jack Run. It was written by my daughter, Ebony and she played the role of a supporting character Jane. The play was about a kid who struggles with high school, home life, and loss and how all those things converge."

"Your daughter wrote it?"

"Yeah, my girls attend a private performing arts school. Ebie writes and acts and Jhené plays the violin."

"And you just have the two?"

"Yep." He stirred the ice in his drink with the straw. "What about you?"

"Oh my God no. I can barely manage my own life. I don't think I could add a child to the mix."

"I get that. I often wonder, how am I the father of two teenagers? Like when the fuck did that happen?"

Leaning forward, I toyed with the initial charm around my necklace. He was easy to talk to. "It's funny when one of my girlfriends tells me they're pregnant, I'm never not in shock. Like yes we're in our thirties and most of them are married or in committed relationships, but a baby? Are you mad?"

"Is that something you eventually want?" A shot of color overtook his face. "I'm sorry that was probably too personal." Justus reached out, briefly touching my arm.

The unexpected physical connection forced me to swallow a moan.

"It's not. I've never met a man that's made me want to birth his big-headed babies. But maybe adoption or a surrogate some time down the line. I froze my eggs to keep my options open." Now it was my turn to apologize. "I'm sorry that was definitely TMI." I don't know what it was about him that made me want to tell him all my deepest and darkest secrets. Outside of Tracie, no one knew I'd opted to preserve my eggs, just in case.

"No apologies needed. It's smart to give yourself options."

I was grateful he didn't judge my decision. I'd lost count of the friends, family, and acquaintances who'd asked me when I was going to get married and start a family. As if the work I was doing wasn't important.

There wasn't only one way to live a fulfilled life. For some people they wanted babies and PTA meetings and others wanted deadlines and board meetings. I was a strong proponent that we should give people space to make the choices that were best for them.

When our food arrived, our conversation mostly consisted of clinking utensils and smacking lips. Halfway through the meal, we exchanged plates and I was delighted by another delicious serving of food. Sharing was a good idea. After greedily cleaning my plate, I wiped at the corners of my mouth with my napkin. "I promise I don't normally consume food like it's my last meal."

"No you're good. It's probably what helps you maintain those healthy curves." Justus cupped his hand over his mouth. His features were shrouded but there was the faintest twitch at the corner of his eye that told me he regretted his words.

This dinner was super informative. I'd learned Justus was single but dating. He was an attentive father who made his girls a priority. And he appreciated the wagon I was dragging. "Do you want to split dessert? I had my eye on the bread pudding."

Justus leaned back in his chair, his gaze both intense and cautious. "I'd like that."

JUSTUS

We were sharing a bowl of caramel croissant bread pudding, and I still didn't know why I was here. When I received her call inviting me to dinner, I immediately thought the worst. Assuming she had not been impressed by my interview on Monday and was hoping to fire me in a neutral location. This restaurant was just the place to do it. It was filled with business professionals commiserating about the workday and couples enjoying romantic meals. Security would promptly escort me out the door and ban me from ever returning if I made a scene in an establishment like this.

But now, sitting across from her as she licked caramel off her spoon with her tongue, I wasn't so sure what her intentions were. This dinner felt like a rendezvous. An entertaining and flirty dalliance. If this were in fact a date, it would be the best I'd had in quite some time. I would already be divining a way to kiss her good night. And when I got home, I'd be counting the days until I could call and ask her out again.

Sariah's toes were playing peek-a-boo into my line of sight from the side of the table. They were painted red and it was all I could do to stop myself from imagining her feet cradling my dick. This woman was beautiful at any distance, but up close she was stunning. I had to wonder what lucky bastard was waking up to that face each morning. Our meeting is strictly business, I reminded myself and I needed her to get to the purpose of our conclave.

The waiter returned with the check.

"Please charge it to penthouse suite twenty-seven with a thirty percent gratuity," Sariah said before I could interject.

"Yes ma'am," the waiter chimed in.

"Whoa, what are you doing? I'm paying," I objected.

She politely waved the waiter away. "No, I invited you to dinner, you don't get to pay."

"I'm going to have to insist." Maybe I was old school but if a woman was with me, she didn't have to pull out her wallet for anything. Even if that woman was a newly minted billionaire.

"You can insist all you want but I've already charged it to my room."

"I'll repay you." I pulled out my wallet.

"I won't accept it. Just allow someone to treat you."

I chuckled. "You're not someone, you're my boss."

"Exactly so don't act like I'm not going to write this dinner off as a business expense."

"To qualify wouldn't we have to discuss business?"

"I'm getting to that."

"Getting to?"

"I was just buttering you up with rich meats and creamy cheeses."

"Buttering me up for what exactly?"

"A business opportunity."

"Are you about to recruit me into some pyramid scheme?"

"No."

"That's a relief because I don't do well with high-pressure sales. I still own a time-share in Florida."

She completely ignored my words and for the first time that night, she appeared nervous. "As you know I've recently inherited a basketball team. What you may not know is I have limited experience overseeing a sports organization. I'm also in need of an introductory basketball course. I was hoping to enlist your help as a consultant. And of course you would be compensated for your time."

"I don't quite follow. I'm the coach."

"Yes and who better than the team's coach to provide insight into the organization." Placing her elbows on the table, she propped her chin onto her hands. "When we met the other day you mentioned there was a disconnect between upper management and the coaching staff. This could be a great opportunity to help chip away at some of that blockage."

"You want me to teach you about basketball. You know they have books for that?"

"I learn better one on one."

Hold up. So she'd invited me to dinner to ask me to be her basketball professor? I was certain if she wanted, she could hire an individual who wasn't me to show her the ins and outs of the sport. My time was spread thin as it was with work, physical therapy, my girls, and trying to squeeze in time for a personal life. I did not have the capacity to show my new boss the ropes.

"Isn't this a task better suited for Busch?" Nolan Busch was the general manager and as such should be Sariah's right-hand man.

"I'm not asking Nolan. I'm asking you."

"Why?"

"Why you or why not Nolan?"

"Either will do."

"Coach Chappel in our brief interactions I have noticed a few things. You're a straight shooter. You don't tell people what they want to hear. And you have a love for this ball club."

My eyes tightened at the corners. "It's not called a ball club. Ball club is a term reserved for baseball."

"See you're a natural teacher. And I am eager to learn." She offered up a smile that made my dick pay attention.

I was willing to teach her a thing or two, but it wouldn't be about basketball. Damnit why couldn't she have asked me to provide sexual education? That was a proposal I would jump at. The last thing I wanted to do was spend overtime working with my boss. Sure helping her out would most likely spare me from the chopping block but I didn't need this albatross weighing me down.

And if I said no, what then?

"What's the goal?" I asked.

"My goal is to have a better understanding of the organization my father dedicated so much of his life to.

And I think it's important to assess a business to properly understand its valuation."

"How long?"

"However long you think it would take, but no longer than three months."

"You want me to teach you the history of the Ramblers' organization and the league as a whole in three months while maintaining my very busy day job and personal life?"

"So are you in?"

"You said there would be compensation?"

"Yes, I'll have my lawyer draw something up."

"My consultation fees are not cheap." I wasn't trying to hustle her, but this was business and I knew my worth. It didn't matter that with the proper motivation I would probably take out her trash, change the oil in her car, and replace all her smoke detector batteries. This was my job and if I was going to impart years of my professional experience that would come at a premium price.

"Feel free to submit a counter offer."

"When would I be expected to start?"

"Once the contract was executed."

Resting back in my chair, I took her measure. Was she serious? She'd interviewed several individuals within the Ramblers' organization and landed on me. Nolan Busch was a longtime family friend of the Thorntons. He always had Grover's back, so I would expect that support to extend to Grover's daughter. Busch was the obvious choice. But Sariah chose me instead. I didn't know if I should be flattered or concerned.

"Deal." I stretched my arm across the table and she slipped her manicured hand in mine. Her grip was strong. And when our hands separated, I could still feel the warmth of her touch. "Did I hear correctly that you're staying at this hotel?"

"Yep, I don't have a place in Vegas."

"Couldn't you just stay at your father's house?"

"No. I didn't inherit the Las Vegas estate and me and my stepmother don't exactly get along."

"Harper Thornton is a different breed. She'd show up to games with this perpetual look, like someone just farted in her beer."

Sariah laughed full and loud. "Why does she always look like that? Even when she smiles it seems painful. I don't know what my father saw in that woman."

"I mean …" I cupped my hands a distance from my chest.

"Are you implying my father was a boobs man?"

"It certainly wasn't the ass and it damn sure wasn't her sour patch face. But I don't know maybe in private she was a witty conversationalist."

"I doubt it."

"What about you and your brother, are you two close?"

"My brother?"

"Yeah the little kid. I think he's around eight."

"Zander. I don't really know him. I live in New York and mostly only saw him when I came to visit for the holidays."

It would appear Sariah's relationship with her old man was more strained than I originally thought. She disliked his second wife and hadn't made much of an effort to get to know her baby brother.

"I couldn't imagine having a sibling I wasn't tight with."

Sariah squared her posture, deliberately uncurling her vertebrae. "We're thirty years apart, what do you expect?"

"I'm not judging. If I had an eight-year-old brother it would be weird … no doubt. But he's still my brother and family is important. Maybe now that you're in town you two can connect."

"I'm not in town." Her tone was defensive. "I'm in Vegas temporarily until I figure out what to do with all this shit my dad just dumped on me."

"So your ultimate goal is to eventually sell the Ramblers?"

"My ultimate goal is none of your fucking business."

Ahh, I see how it is. Now that the deal was done out came the real Sariah. All claws and gnashing teeth. I was just trying to make conversation. I wasn't looking to get my head chewed off. She was my boss and this was a business transaction and I'd do well to remember that. No need to get too familiar.

I leaned back in my chair. "Are we done here? Because I'm getting the sense we're done."

She jerked her shoulders into a shrug.

"You have a good night Ms. Thornton," I said, pushing away from the table and exiting the restaurant headed toward the lobby.

"Dad," Jhené whined.

"No."

"You just can't say no," Ebony said.

"Ebie you and your sister are fourteen. You are not going to an XYZ Baby concert."

"Rap is a form of music and music is art," Jhené chimed in.

"Well his music is not suitable for a fourteen-year-old. Whatever happened to Mimi Starr?"

"You can't be serious," Ebony said.

All I knew was that Mimi Starr made songs about dancing, embracing who you were, and cruising the mall with your friends. XYZ Baby rapped about three-somes, drugs, and killing people. My girls could be mad at me for a few days, but I was their father and it was my job to protect them.

Because I traveled a lot, my time with my kids was sacred. The days I had them I made sure to see them off to school and, when I was able, pick them up. My two girls were at the age where they would soon be hanging out with friends without the supervision of adults. It was important our girls knew they were loved and that Mom and Dad had their backs. I also hoped we'd equipped them with the tools they would need to maneuver through their teen years.

"What do you think Uncle Deck?" Jhené asked.

"I'm staying all the way out of this," Deck said.

I flashed him a look of approval. As a father to a college-age daughter, he understood how taxing raising children could be.

"Can we get some ice cream?" Ebie asked, her hand

already outstretched for cash because she knew her old man was a softie.

I watched them jump in line. It was Saturday and we were at the farmers' market looking for vegetables for tonight's dinner. The girls also talked me into getting them matching forever bracelets from a jewelry vendor. Deck called when we were headed out the door and agreed to join us.

Despite the occasional interruption from a fan asking for Deck's autograph, we were having a good time. I'd known Deck for years. We were rivals and then teammates. I retired after a knee injury that I never fully recovered from and moved on to coaching. When we were on the court, I held Deck accountable just like any other player. Off the court I considered him one of my closest friends.

"I'm still tripping over the fact that Thornton is gone. I didn't like the man but I sure as hell didn't wish death on him," he said.

"Life comes at you fast."

"And apparently death comes even quicker."

"Ain't that the truth."

As if a light bulb illuminated over his head, Deck asked, "What happened at your dinner date with big boss Sariah?"

"Definitely wasn't a date." Raising my hand to my temple, I attempted to shield my eyes. I was a decent liar, but every now and then Deck caught me slipping. "It was a complete nothing burger. She just had some follow-up questions. What do you think about X. Can I get your thoughts on Y."

I pointed to an empty bench where we could sit and still keep an eye out on the twins. A nagging sharp pain was aggravating my knee and getting off my feet for a few was my primary objective. Lowering myself to the bench, I grumbled and groaned just like my seventy-six-year-old father did whenever he sat.

Deck noticed and asked. "You good?"

"Yeah, you know me."

"I do. You're the type who thinks he needs to push through the pain instead of taking it easy or asking for help."

"What are you going to offer me a piggyback ride?" I joked.

"No, I'm not carrying your big ass. But you could've mentioned you needed to rest."

"I don't need to rest. I'm fine." My features hardened. Talking about my health was something I tried to avoid. I used to be able to rely on my body to do exactly what I wanted it to. Now at forty-four with pins in my left knee, my body often betrayed me. Most times I could push through the pain, it was more annoying than anything else. But there were occasions when the intense throbbing and cramp like stiffness would practically bring me to tears.

"No the fuck you're not. You're in pain. Just because you put on a brave face don't think I can't tell you're hurting."

"It's just something I have to live with."

"Did you call that doctor Pratt referred you to?"

"She's not a doctor, she's a surgeon. Didn't you ask me a question about Sariah?"

"Oh so now you want to talk about boss babe?"

"Rather talk about that instead of the bullshit you're on. Listen, the team needs to focus on the mission. It doesn't matter who the owner is, the objective is always to win every game or leave it all on the court trying to."

"You ain't gotta tell me that. Shit, I know that but some of these other motherfuckers, not so much."

"What are they saying?"

"Some of the guys have been vocal about preferring a trade rather than be on a team owned by a woman."

"That's stupid. The checks clear all the same."

"I don't have no problems working for a woman. I support it. I have a daughter of my own. My issue with Ms. Thornton is I don't believe she gives two fucks about the Ramblers. And when she's done conducting interviews and shuffling files around, she's going to sell us to the highest bidder. So don't get used to her pretty face because it's not going to be around for very long."

Deck wasn't wrong. Sariah had a trust problem. Players didn't believe she held their best interest at heart. And when a player felt unappreciated or under-valued, that's when they started looking for somewhere else to call home. My players trusted me, but that trust would only reach so far. I needed to get Sariah up to speed immediately if I wanted to maintain our momentum.

"We're just going to have to let this shit play out. In the meantime as a veteran I expect you to remain level headed. You've come a long way from the Deck of a few years ago."

"I intend to keep my nose clean and my shooting hand hot." Deck cracked his knuckles.

I scanned the area for the girls who had moved from the ice cream stand to a vintage shirt vendor. When I turned my attention back to Deck, he was eyeing me. "What fool?"

Deck rubbed his palms together. "So … Sloane has a friend. Maybe we could set up a double date."

"Is this you talking or Sloane?"

"You know that woman considers you family and she would like you to get laid every now and again." Deck held up his hands. "Her words, not mine."

"Listen, I don't need any help in the dating department. And as for sex I'm doing fine."

"Okay, but Sloane showed me a picture of her friend. You know I had to verify and she's a baddie."

"If she's got Sloane's fiery personality, I think I'll pass."

"My baby is a handful." Deck lowered his voice to a whisper. "Last night she had my balls in a vise grip and was just beating my meat. Can men squirt?"

My face crumpled in disgust. "I'm pretty sure that was just regular old piss."

"Are you sure because it tasted—"

"Stop talking to me about your freaky ass sex life." I shook my head, hoping to escape his oversharing.

"Sorry. Maybe if you were getting laid you wouldn't be so uptight."

I wasn't uptight, but it was one in the afternoon and I didn't want to talk about sex acts at the local farmers' market with my kids a stone's throw away. Just because

I didn't have a girlfriend, it didn't mean I wasn't actively having sex. You could definitely have one without the other.

"So it's a no on the blind date. What about Sariah? Boss lady is fine as hell."

"Okay." My shoulder hopped. Surely he wasn't suggesting Sariah as a potential romantic partner.

"Don't act like you didn't notice. She's also your type."

"She's attractive I'll give you that. But she's our boss and she's also a distraction."

I shared most things with Deck but after reviewing the contract Sariah's lawyers emailed over, I thought it best to keep our arrangement close to the vest. The terms were generous but the crux of the document was about discretion and confidentiality. So I should try to not break the agreement before the work even began. Speaking of work, I would spend the remainder of the weekend gathering documents and creating Ramblers 101 binders for our lessons. I even assembled a glossary of the most popular sports terms. By the time I was through, she would be well versed in basketball, the NBA, and Ramblers' Nation.

SARIAH

Justus showed up to my place ready to teach. He must have headed to my suite straight from work because he was still in his suit. For the past few days, I'd been hyping myself up for our first session. People always said I had the attention span of a three-year-old child because I was so easily distracted. That was probably Tracie's biggest gripe about me because she had to repeat information several times before I actually processed it.

"This place is nice. I didn't realize they had actual condos." Justus set the banker's box he was carrying down next to the couch. "Did it come fully furnished?"

"Yes, which made it the best choice. If I had to spend time picking out furniture and reviewing fabric swatches this place would just contain two folding chairs and a hodgepodge of pillows.

"Well they did a good job. It doesn't feel like a hotel."

"I ordered some food so I hope you're hungry." Our last meeting ended on a tense note. The food was my way of apologizing for being so blunt. Justus struck a nerve. My current situation didn't resemble a happy blended family like The Fresh Prince of Bel-Air. The Thornton clan wouldn't be gathering for backyard barbeques or doing the cha cha slide any time soon.

Justus followed me to the kitchen. "Oh yeah, what did you get?"

"Greek food," I said, pulling containers out of a bag.

Washing his hands in the sink, he asked, "Plates?"

"Last cabinet on the right."

"Did you have a good day?"

The way he floated around the kitchen felt familiar. Like we were a committed couple who'd been together for years and made it a point to have dinners together. Commiserating over work and laughing about the lighter spots in our day.

"It was good. I had a ton of meetings. Between the Ramblers and then meetings for the skincare launch."

"Skincare launch?"

He asked a lot of questions. Initially, I took it as a sign he was being presumptuous. But now I think he was just genuinely curious. That or he was just as nervous as I was and chose to fill any potential silence with word vomit.

"My beauty company is launching a new line of products in a few months. In preparation, there are tons of strategy sessions with my team."

"I would imagine that keeps you busy … on top of everything else." He dished rice onto the plates.

"It does. What about your day?"

Breath exited his lungs in a quick whoosh. "I have

this new boss. And she's kind of put everyone at work on edge."

"She must be a real bitch."

Justus's chestnut eyes landed on me. His gaze was always charged as if he was taking inventory of my soul. "That's the thing. She doesn't seem like a bitch. I mean I'm sure she can be, but not without cause." He reached over me to grab the tongs.

"Nice to hear you giving me the benefit of the doubt."

He pointed at the plate. "Do you want salad?"

"Yes." He loaded leafy greens onto the plate before handing it to me. "Thank you." This man just made my plate. Considering my needs before his. The men I've dated recently all wanted to be catered to. Despite being an entrepreneur they expected me to fill a traditional role. I am not the traditional Suzy homemaker type. Maybe the bar was in hell, but Justus's simple act prickled my face into a blush. Heading to the dining table, I waited for him to join me.

He arrived with his plate and two glasses of wine, placing one in front of me.

"So what's in the box?" I pointed to the banker's box near the couch.

"That is your study material."

"Are you serious?"

"There's a lot of information to remember and you look like a visual learner." He cut into his chicken, taking a bite.

He was correct I did learn best with visual aids. If you told me something, I'd one hundred percent forget.

But if you showed me, preferably with pictures or a slide show accompanied by a fun antidote, I would be able to recall it for the rest of my life.

"Nice to see you're taking this assignment seriously."

"You're paying me so I want to make sure you get your money's worth." He brought a spoonful of rice to his mouth.

"I just want to reiterate that what we're doing here should remain between me and you."

"Don't worry, I'm not going to tell everyone you're attending the Chappel Night School for Wayward Souls."

"Thank you, I appreciate it. I'm not ashamed about needing help getting up to speed. I just don't want others to perceive me as inept."

"I think it takes a lot of balls to admit you need help. I've worked for a lot of people … coaches and GM's who didn't know what the fuck they were doing and were too arrogant to ask for assistance. I've been in the business of basketball for over twenty years and I still ask people I respect for advice. Learning is a part of living and it's life long."

"Before we get into the history of the organization … tell me about yourself." My request was a selfish one. I enjoyed listening to the robust timbre of his voice and I wouldn't mind getting to know him better.

"You should really Google me. I'm kind of a big deal." A smirk slid up one half of his face.

"I was waiting to hear it from the horse's mouth."

"Fair enough. I went to the University of North

Carolina."

"Basketball scholarship?"

"No, I just got into UNC off of my grades. And then the second week of school they held open tryouts for the basketball team. Any Joe Blow could sign up. I did and got picked. By the middle of freshman year I was a starter." He narrowed his eyes and continued, "A starter is a player that—"

"I know what a starter is. Thank you very much."

"Good so you're not as bad off as I feared." He winked.

Amusement enlivened my eyes. "Did you play ball in high school?"

"I did but I wasn't good enough to get recruited."

"What changed?"

He shrugged. "Maybe my dedication changed. I realized I could make real money in the league even if it was only for a few years. That money could help fund other business ventures."

"Such as?"

"I own a few restaurants. A Fat Burger, Sweet Greens, and a couple Chick-fil-A's."

"A restaurant franchise can be lucrative."

"It's expensive to get into but the projected revenue can make you millions."

"After college?"

"I got drafted in the first round and ended up signing with the Timberwolves."

"First round? So that means you were pretty good."

"I wasn't Colin Pratt but I was decent."

"What made you decide to retire?"

He tapped his left knee, giving it a rub. "I got injured and had to have surgery. I was fine for a while but eventually got injured again … same knee."

I could listen to this man talk all night. His voice was deep and husky, and when words left his mouth, the reverb seemed to linger in the air for a bit before dissipating. He talked with his hands. Slicing the air or pushing some nonexistent object out of the way. I was mostly stricken with how relaxed he seemed. As if we were friends just catching up over a meal. I appreciated that he was comfortable around me.

When he entered the suite, he'd removed his shoes and jacket. Eventually, he loosened his tie and rolled up his sleeves. A man in a button down with the sleeves rolled up was probably one of the sexiest looks a man could rock. Each time he flexed, I could see his muscles threatening to burst free from the checkered patterned shirt like the Incredible Hulk. His forearms also grabbed my attention at the sight of the strong veins that lined his arm.

"So you went into coaching college basketball. Is that correct?"

He nodded. Taking a break from talking to pull a cube of lamb from the skewer before popping it in his mouth.

"Did you enjoy it?"

"I loved it. There's just something about being around young men who have their entire lives ahead of them and being able to help them navigate the world around them." His eyes came alive when he talked.

"So you enjoy the role of mentor."

He leaned back in his chair, pinning his arms across his chest. "When do I get to ask questions?"

"What do you want to know?"

"Tell me about your business ... your beauty business."

A warm smile stretched across my face. I loved talking about my company, but in day-to-day conversations people rarely asked me about it. When I introduced myself to someone new, nine times out of ten, they'd ask, "Any relation to Grover Thornton?" And I'd have to say he's my father. Once people knew that, they were more interested in talking about him or my experience of him as a parent.

"I started the company when I was twenty-eight after years of bouncing from one interest to another. My friend Tracie, she's my business partner, she worked in the beauty industry at one of those legacy makeup brands. We were both Black women and even though our complexions were on different ends of the spectrum, we each found it difficult identifying foundation, blush, and lipsticks that complemented our skin tones."

"So you created a company that would."

"Exactly." I smiled sheepishly.

"My wife swears by your products. The only thing that touches her face."

"Your wife?" My chest panged with disappointment.

"Ex-wife."

"How long has she been your ex?"

"Long enough for me to not still be referring to her as my wife. Anyway, I've heard of Genuine Beauty and the women I know go up for your products."

"Thanks. I'm proud of what we created." I should have left it there but I couldn't help myself. "What happened with you and your wife? If you don't mind me asking."

"I do mind." He stood collecting our plates. "I think that's enough Q and A for one night."

Empty glasses in hand, I followed him to the kitchen. Justus washed the dishes while I placed the leftover food containers in the fridge. Classic Sariah. Things would be going well and then I'd say or do something to muck it all up. Why did I think Justus would want to talk about his ex-wife with me? Whatever happened to cause the demise of their relationship was none of my business. Shit, maybe he still held a soft spot for her and was hoping for a reconciliation.

"Let's get to work," he said, folding the damp dish towel.

I grabbed a plate of brownie bites and followed him to the couch. "So what's first, Coach?"

He removed a thick binder from the banker's box and placed it onto my lap. Tapping on the front of my binder, he said, "Let's look at the topics I intend to cover. If you think something is missing let me know." Reaching into the box once more, he pulled out a duplicate binder to my own.

"When did you have time to do all this?"

"I enlisted my two girls to help me put together the binders. Great family bonding time."

"Do your girls live with you?"

He spread assorted pens and highlighters on the coffee table. "Their mother and I share custody. We live ten minutes from one another so we switch off weeks." He opened his binder and motioned for me to do the same. "So let's talk about the Ramblers' organization per Grover Thornton."

Once we cracked the binders open, he was pretty much all business. Outlining how the team was established, their ties to Vegas and the original owners who were rumored to be gangsters. I tried my best to follow along, highlighting sections he emphasized as vital information. About halfway through my introductory lesson, I'd been reduced to rapid head nods to signify I was following along.

When I released a big yawn, Justus stopped to comment. "Am I boring you?"

"A little bit yeah. I thought basketball in Vegas would be a little more … sexy. Other than the mob ties it's been kind of a snoozefest."

Justus shut his binder and rubbed his eyes. "I warned you it was a lot of information. But you need to know how things started so you can appreciate where the team is currently at."

"And I respect your thorough retelling. It's just I think dinner is sending me into a food coma."

Justus stood, shaking out his long limbs. His first steps were timid and a bit stiff. He groaned faintly as he made his way over to the floor to ceiling windows. "This is a really nice view. At night you forget how basic this city is. The lights have a mesmerizing effect."

I joined him at the window. "I used to think the Vegas lights were a shield. Guarding the residents as they made their way through the night."

Justus flashed me a skeptical eye.

"I was ten at the time and into comic books."

"This city has definitely swallowed whole those who veer too far from the protection of the lights."

"Not a Vegas fan?"

"I always say this city is a great place to visit."

"Spoken like a true transplant." I nudged my shoulder into his side.

"Sorry, I'm a small-town boy. When I retire it will be to a vast plot of land far away from others."

"Don't tell me you're an antisocial introvert."

"Oh, I like maybe seven people. The rest I could do without."

"Ouch."

"I'm open to expanding the roster but that person would have to be ten over ten."

"I'll keep that in mind."

Justus glanced at me, slightly taken aback. "What are you looking for a spot in my top seven?" His tone was jovial.

As his boss we would probably be breaking some rule, but the cynical coach piqued my interest. Not many men could accomplish that. I was fully entrenched in my soft girl era, with work that fulfilled me, friends who supported me, and family who reminded me who I was and where I came from. Any type of relationship with Justus would complicate things. Maybe I was a glutton for punishment or just extremely horny, because right now all I wanted to do was feel his body pressed against mine. "Justus?"

He turned to look at me once again, the smile fading

from his face when he recognized the hunger in my gaze. It wasn't too late to walk this back and pretend I wasn't totally willing to blur the lines between work and personal. But my feet were affixed to the floor, unable to retreat. I wanted him and I wanted him to show me he wanted me. We stood mere inches from one another. His hand brushed the side of my arm causing my muscles to flex. Justus leaned closer and the warmth of his breath tickled my face.

"Am I reading the room correctly?" he asked.

"I don't know. What are you picking up?"

He tilted his head and said, "I'm thinking you want to be fucked. But I could be wrong."

My heart was devising its escape from my chest with each beat faster than the next. The way he was looking at me sent shivers down the length of my spine. His stare encapsulated the manner in which a man looks at a woman when everything is new and the future unknown.

"Yes, that is exactly what I want."

The corner of his mouth ticked upward, and he closed the scant distance between us with a kiss. He wasn't in a hurry. The slow slide of his tongue told me he wanted to savor me. Justus's hand grazed my torso on the way to cupping my face and goose pimples appeared on my skin. His lips tasted spicy and sweet, a mixture of dinner and dessert.

His faint breath was measured and slow, unlike mine, which had grown ragged. When his eyelashes fluttered, they tickled my face. I'd noticed upon our first meeting he had beautiful long lashes and I was a smidge jealous. My hand came to rest on his chest. His body was rocklike as if carved out of stone, but the warmth that emanated off him told me different.

He pulled away and I thought he'd come to his senses. But the look in his eyes told a different story. Towering over me, he bit his lip, taking a step forward causing me to take steps back. We continued like this until my back was pressed against the window. This time when he kissed me it was like he was trying to destroy my mouth. Like he'd decided to prove he was all in. I moaned in pleasure at his longing for me. The bristles of his beard scratched at my face, but I placed my hand firmly on the back of his head, begging for more. Our tongues worked back and forth, dipping in and out of the other's mouth.

Justus's fingers were on my blouse undoing the buttons. I helped him tug off my shirt, sending it floating to the floor. He plunged his face into my breast, kissing the lace of my bra then licking upward until he landed on my chin. His massive hands slid to my ass, and he lifted me off the ground like my five-foot ten-inch frame was a mere rag doll.

Nipping at his lips, I wanted to make him feel both pleasure and pain until he begged me for sweet release. My body shuddered when an image of him fucking me from behind flashed into my head. I dipped my tongue into his mouth with sloppy wet kisses. A shrill ringing from a phone punctured the air, but I ignored it, everything else could wait. Unfortunately, Justus didn't feel the same way. With one final kiss he pulled away, our mouths still connected by a thread of saliva.

With a tap to my backside he said, "I have to answer that."

I dropped my legs and my bare feet landed on the floor. Justus was already across the room, fishing his phone from his jacket pocket. Answering the call, he moved out of earshot. It was like I was in limbo, my entire being on pause waiting for him to return to me.

Back in the room, he said, "I gotta go."

I know the expression on my face told him I thought he'd lost his damn mind. He moved closer, causing my body to practically hum with anticipation. "I don't want you to go."

"I can see that." He rubbed his palm over the erect nipple that was pressing against my bra. "It's my girls. Their mother has to work late. So I have daddy duty."

I picked up my blouse from the floor. "Of course. I completely understand. I mean what the hell were we doing anyway." Grabbing the plate of brownie bites, I placed the leftovers in a Ziploc bag. "You should give them these."

"Thank you." His fingers brushed mine.

"Great first lesson. Super informative."

His eyes narrowed and he seemed to examine my face. Turning away, he rushed to gather his stuff. "Have a good night."

"Yep. I'm going to spend the remainder of the evening reviewing all this material." What I actually did once he left was place my vibrator on the highest setting and imagine the silicone was his hard dick.

JUSTUS

AM I STUPID OR AM I DUMB? I'M NOT SURE WHICH category I fall into, but kissing Sariah Thornton was some dimwitted shit. In my defense, the woman smelled like sex and had pouty, full lips that begged to be kissed, sucked, and, if I'd had the chance, fucked. But now in the stark light of day, I was able to admit it was a mistake. For so many reasons, primarily of which was the fact that she was essentially my boss.

There was no written rule forbidding a relationship between an owner and a coach. In a handful of cases, sports team owners engaged in public relationships with some even getting hitched. Despite that fact, it was still considered taboo and I always tried to avoid relationships with women who worked for or closely with the organization. It was best to steer clear of the inevitable drama.

I had no clue what Sariah was looking for. Maybe she wanted to explore the physical attraction that we both felt. It was there from our first smoke at her father's repast. At the time I didn't make much of it. She was grieving and I was doing my best not to get distracted by her baby smooth hands. Maybe she was just looking to get her back blown out and hoped I was up to the task. Trust me I was, and she would not be disappointed.

Not that any of that mattered. I was going to have to put the kibosh on the whole affair and make it clear I was only here in a mentor capacity. And Sariah would just have to accept it or she could fire me. Of course after I made this platonic declaration, I would need to let go of any ideas of her scraping her nails down my back while I spread her wide. Why couldn't she have been born with an unfortunate face? And looked more like her daddy and less like my dream woman right down to the cupid's bow.

"Slow it down Pratt, no need to rush," Klay, my assistant coach yelled from beside me, pulling me from my thoughts.

The team was in the middle of a practice working on passing and shooting drills. It was a Friday and we had a Saturday game, but the players were sluggish. Less hustle. It was my job to keep them motivated, but my head was still in that penthouse suite even though my feet were firmly planted on the wood floors.

McCabe passed the ball to Pratt who dribble fake pumped and passed the ball to Adeyemi, at which point the play seemed to fall apart with the players attention being drawn to something behind me. I turned to determine the cause of the disruption and spotted Sariah walking in with the president of business operations and the senior basketball advisor. Her visit was unexpected, and I wished someone had given me a courtesy heads up. A murmur buzzed through the gymnasium as the players took note of our special guests.

I clapped my hands. "Hey, focus gentlemen. Practice is far from over."

"Hello Coach Chappel. The team is looking good," Morgan Clark, the basketball advisor said.

I forced a smile. "What are you guys doing here? I typically only see you in the skybox."

"We were coming back from a business lunch and Sariah mentioned she'd never seen the practice space."

Sariah moved forward offering a reserved smile. "Coach Chappel, very nice to see you again." Her words were distant and cold like her tongue wasn't sucking and licking mine just two nights prior.

"Welcome to the Ramblers training center Ms. Thornton," I said.

"Please call me Sariah. How long does practice typically run?"

"It depends on the game schedule. We can have up to two practices a day for about three hours each. I prefer earlier morning practice but that doesn't always work out."

Sariah turned her attention to the players running drills across the court. Even in her casual business attire, she couldn't hide her sexy side. She was wearing a gray and black striped suit with an asymmetrical jacket. The way she styled it was fresh and different, signifying someone who had their own unique sense of what worked well on their body. Even though the suit was neutral, the way she wore it was not. This was a woman who garnered attention when she entered a room, I knew she had mine.

The chance to lay eyes on that stunning woman didn't change the reality that I hated surprise visits even more so when it was from executive management. Their goal was to make money, which I completely understood. But the way they viewed the players as cattle that could be bought and sold at will was disturbing. For me, money didn't even make my top five list of priorities. I was responsible for the men on my team. Their mental, physical, and emotional well-being was important to me. Maybe because I was once a player and understood the toll the league could extract.

"Keep your eye on the ball. How'd you miss that," I yelled at a player administering tough love.

As the two executives talked with my assistant coach, I ambled over to Sariah who was standing a few feet away. My goal was to gauge her temperature on what transpired between us.

"So what do you think?" I pointed in the direction of the court.

"They look strong, and they're working as a cohesive team." She let out an exhausted sigh. "I don't fucking know. All I've talked about all morning is basketball and the business of the sport. At this point my brain feels like jelly."

"That kind of comes with owning a sports team. People want to talk about the sport."

"I'm going to let you in on a little secret Coach Chappel, there's more to life than sports."

I frowned at her use of my title and last name.

"What?"

I looked back to make sure the two paper pushers were still engrossed in conversation with Klay. "You called me Coach Chappel."

"That's your name."

"Why so formal? It's just you and me."

"I'm being professional. What would you have me call you?"

Daddy, baby, a dirty boy. Shit, she could call me a nasty slut while she sucked my dick from behind, anything but Coach Chappel.

I leaned in a little closer, not as close as I wanted to be, but close enough to smell the spicy floral scent of her skin that was driving me wild. "I prefer Justus."

"Justus," she repeated after me.

"That's a good start. I'd like to hear you say it a little softer with a bit of breathiness behind it."

The thing about me was when I wanted something, I worked hard to obtain it. And in that moment, with her flirty hair toss and mysterious mink eyes, I realized just how much I wanted Sariah. Was I shooting my shot? Definitely. This was my chance to let her know what happened the other night didn't have to be a one off.

Now Justus, weren't you just saying sex with Sariah would be a mistake and you needed to keep shit professional? Yes, but I was lying. I had no intentions of being work acquaintances with this woman. Not when she was looking up at me like she was imagining me naked.

She parted her perfect mouth to speak but before she could, a ball came flying in our direction and directly toward Sariah's head. I grabbed hold of her arm in an attempt to remove her from the line of fire but the ball still managed to tag her on the back. She grimaced in pain and was forced to take a knee.

I reached out to steady her. "Are you okay?"

"Yep, it's fine, just knocked the wind out of me." She forced a smile.

Standing, I directed my anger at the ball thrower. "Dexter, what the fuck is wrong with you?"

"Sorry coach, it just got away from me." His tawny face looked like all the blood had been drained from it.

"Laps now," I yelled at the entire team.

Turning my attention back to Sariah I helped her to her feet. "I'm going to get her an ice pack," I said, to Klay leaving him behind to babysit the two execs. On the way to my office, I grabbed an ice pack and handed it to her.

"If you want we can have the doc check it out."

She removed her jacket and struggled to angle the ice pack on her lower back.

"Give it to me," I instructed, guiding her until she was leaning on my desk. I stood in front of her and rested the ice pack on the lower half of her back.

She winced, digging her fingers into my shoulder. "It's sore and cold."

I readjusted and once I found a position that caused her not to cringe. I didn't move.

"It's official," I said.

"What is?"

"You're not a part of the team until you get pegged by the ball."

"Do I get a tank top with my number on it?"

"It's a jersey," I replied in horrified shock. "How do you not know that?"

She shrugged one shoulder. I noticed that even though we were face to face, her gaze settled on everything in the room except me.

"You're a trooper. That ball hit you pretty hard, I'm surprised you didn't cry."

"I'm not a big fan of crying."

"Once when I got hit in the head with a ball. My ear was ringing and it felt like someone scrambled my brain. I didn't cry, it was more of a whimper."

She moved and I dropped the ice pack. Sariah pulled the side of her silky tank up trying to assess the damage.

"How does it look?" she asked.

I ran my hand over her bare skin. She seeped in air, reacting to my touch or maybe it was because of the pain. "It's definitely going to leave a bruise. When you get home, you should probably apply some heat for the soreness." I needed to place some space between us, so I moved behind my desk.

"Thanks Coach."

I eyed my door, dropping my voice to a whisper. "When do you want to meet up again to … study?"

"Umm, actually I'm heading to the airport after work."

"Back to New York?"

"Yeah, it's a quick trip. I return to Vegas Sunday afternoon."

"Sounds like fun."

GM Busch entered my office in a huff. "There you are. I heard you were hit by a wayward ball. Are you alright?" His voice was dripping with concern.

"Yeah, Coach Chappel nursed me back to health. He gave me an ice pack."

"Hopefully Coach Chappel will also give the team a swift talking to. This is a professional ball league not a pickup game at the park."

"It was an accident," Sariah and I said in unison.

Ignoring both of us, he asked. "Are you feeling up to attending the monthly briefing?"

"Yes, I've been looking forward to it all day. Lead the way," Sariah said, tugging her suit jacket back on.

The two exited my office and I was finally able to relax. Practice would be over in a few minutes, so I decided to let Klay handle it without me. I plopped into my office chair and pulled out my team playbook. We had a home game tomorrow and I still needed to coordinate a few new plays.

I had hoped Sariah and I could pick up where we left off this Saturday. With my dick on hard and her moaning into my mouth. Maybe her leaving for the weekend was for the best. I was actively thinking with my dick and needed some time to clear my head. When she returned, I would do my best to keep it professional, but if she batted her long lashes in my direction, all bets were off.

I'd been locked away in my office for a few hours reviewing game playback when there was a knock on my door. "Busch, twice in one day. What's going on?"

Normally Nolan Busch never left the sanctuary of the executive offices; with the catered food, freezing AC, and private parking. Any time he made an appearance at the training center, it was usually to complain or ask for a favor.

GM Busch closed the door, taking a seat. "I know you're busy Justus, so I'll get to the point."

Please, I thought. I disliked it when people talked around a topic instead of just laying things out plain.

"What is your take on Sariah?"

I shrugged. "I haven't really spent enough time with her to have a take. Why?"

"I think the girl's in over her head."

"Why do you say that?"

"Grover and I were good friends. We talked. Occasionally he mentioned his daughter. She hates basketball and blamed it for her parents' divorce or something. She never came to any of the games although he extended the invitation. And now she is given all of this and doesn't have a clue what to do with it."

"Thornton was a smart man. If he thought it would be a problem he wouldn't have left the team to her." When it came to the Ramblers, Thornton was shrewd. If he left the team under Sariah's care, he must have had his reasons. I think Nolan was pissed he wasn't named as the successor. He was Thornton's second in command. And as I understood it, Nolan had the seal of approval, he was just waiting for the keys to the kingdom.

Busch looked back at the door to confirm it was

closed. "What if I told you Derek Wayne expressed interest in purchasing the team?"

I leaned forward in my seat. "Derek Wayne … five championship rings, three MVP trophies, carried his entire team on his back … Derek Wayne?"

"Yep, and he's enlisted a group of investors who are looking to do the same thing here in Vegas."

I was heady at the thought of having someone who truly loved basketball and understood the game as owner of the Ramblers. It was always a gamble with a new owner, but I was confident Wayne would appreciate some of my ideas and vision for the team. "For that to happen though Sariah would have to sell."

"Maybe if I help her see this isn't a good fit she'll throw in the towel." Nolan picked up a frame on my desk, admiring my twins. "Your player should have thrown the ball at her fucking head, maybe it would have knocked some sense into her." He chuckled.

I clenched my fist under the desk. My face must have displayed the anger that was rippling inside me at his words.

"Lighten up Chappel, it was a joke." He carelessly returned the frame atop my desk.

"She could have been really hurt so let's not joke about it."

He raised his hands apologetically. "My bad I didn't realize you were so sensitive. Anyway, as the coach you may hear some things from the players or others. I would appreciate it if you let me know if anything interesting blows your way."

"Gossip?"

"Yeah, something that can bury the bitch." He offered a smug smirk. "I'm hoping I can gain her trust and convince her to sell. But if that doesn't work, I'll take a sex scandal, a drug addiction, or a freaky fetish." He tapped his knuckles on my desk before heading to the door. "Oh and Justus it should go without saying but let's keep this between you and me. Thanks."

SARIAH

Tracie and I were enjoying food and drinks in a restaurant in Tribeca. When I moved to New York after college, I bounced around different neighborhoods trying to find the right fit. I eventually settled on Tribeca. The area had amazing dining options, tons of shopping, and there was so much to do without ever having to leave the triangle.

We were lucky to find an empty tabletop at Mink's. The place was packed and boisterous. The New York Knicks were in Vegas playing the Ramblers. Every television in the bar was tuned to the game.

"I hope the Knicks win," Tracie said, squeezing spicy sauce onto her taco.

"Hey, that's my team 'you're rooting against. Ramblers Nation baby." I took a swig of my beer.

"Not going to lie that coach of yours can ram my nation anytime." Tracie giggled.

The side of my eye twitched and I pressed my mouth into a thin line.

"What was that?"

"What was what?" I asked innocently.

"The thing you just did with your face."

I plastered on a fake smile. "You're seeing things."

"Sariah, I know you better than anyone. You just did that thing you do when you have news you're not sure you want to share."

"What news would I have to share? I'm always working, no time for fun."

"Yeah, exactly so …" She gasped and pointed an accusatory finger at me. "Does this have anything to do with that fine ass coach?"

I tried to keep my facial expression blank, but Tracie knew me too well.

"Spill it sister."

I dropped my voice to a whisper and leaned closer. "We kind of kissed."

"Of course you did. Because no man can resist the wiles of Sariah Thornton."

"It just happened. Neither one of us expected it."

"Is he a good kisser?"

"Yes, like curl your toes and soak your panties good."

"All you did was kiss?"

"Yes." I decided to leave out the fact that I wanted more and the next time we were alone together I was going to make it clear he could have me anywhere and anyway he wanted. Look, I was well aware I was in a position of power over Justus. As owner of the Ramblers, I was basically his boss. The last thing I wanted to do was become the female Harvey Weinstein. Workplace romances were tricky, which is why I avoided them.

But Justus was giving off big "risk it all" vibes. It was clear he was interested in exploring this chemistry between us. Which made this a no brainer. He was handsome with sculpted muscles. His gait was self-assured, hinting at a man who was used to getting his way. And most importantly he was financially stable. Which, with my newfound windfall, was a plus.

"Boyfriend potential?" Tracie asked.

"Tracie, it was just a kiss. Plus the last thing I need is a man to further complicate my life."

"It doesn't have to be complicated."

Right now, spending time with Justus was anything but complicated. We were effortless together like we'd known one another for years. I first noticed it at the park over a shared spliff and again at the restaurant. It's rare to encounter a person who makes me comfortable enough to let my guard down. Justus had the singular ability to make me feel safe. I confided in two people, my mom and Tracie. Something about that man made me inclined to trust him. And that unassailable security made me want to be vulnerable while nestled in his arms after we fucked one another silly.

"Guess who called me," I said, hoping to change the subject.

Tracie narrowed her eyes, not happy for the topic swap. "Who?" she asked around a mouth full of food.

"Harper."

"For what?"

"She left me a message saying she wanted to talk to me and asked if I could come over for lunch one day next week."

"Are you going to go?"

"Yeah. What was I supposed to do? Say my dad is dead bitch and so is any relationship you and I once had."

Tracie shook her head. "I bet this is about the will. She looked none too pleased at the reading. Shit if someone left me a hundred million dollars. I would never have another complaint for the remainder of my life."

"A hundred million for ten years of work isn't too shabby."

"Well I mean she did have to fuck your dad."

"Don't, I do not want that image in my head. My parents are virgins and I was conceived through immaculate conception."

"Now wait a minute. For an older gentleman your dad was still attractive. I bet your pops was giving Harper the business."

"That may be true but I don't need the details."

Harper and I had never gotten along. In my opinion she was a ditz. Admittedly, when my father first introduced us, I was a brat. She was younger than me by several years. My father was an attractive older man, but the only thing a twenty-something could possibly be interested in was his money and power. If my dad believed Harper loved him, then that was his one blind spot. Harper loved the fancy trips, expensive restaurants, and lavish gifts.

She and I had zero common interest and only spent time together during the holidays. I wasn't interested in getting to know my step mommy and my father's death didn't change that. In her call to me, she mentioned the word family. Harper was not part of my family. She was essentially the woman who was fucking my father for his money, nothing more, nothing less.

"If she brings up the will. Which I'm certain she will. What are you going to say?"

"Do you think she'd press me for a bigger piece of the pie?"

"Yes."

"Shouldn't she be in mourning or something? Dressed in all black, tooling around the house occasionally weeping."

"It's easier to mourn with a coffer filled with cash. You should know that."

My eyebrows climbed up my forehead. "What's that supposed to mean?"

"It means you inherited a substantial chunk of change. And I haven't seen you cry or express any real emotion since this all went down."

I squared my shoulders and elongated my spine ready to fight. "Why is everyone expecting for me to fall apart?" It was true I still hadn't cried since my father died. A month had passed since his death and I was beyond bracing myself, waiting for the emotional shoe to drop. I was fine. And I felt horrible about the fact that I was fine. Horrible knowing I didn't miss him. But I'd accepted that the tears weren't coming.

"No, not fall apart. But maybe you should talk through your feelings with a professional."

"That's what I have you for," I joked, hoping to lighten the mood. The last thing I needed was to talk to someone. My father was absent for most of my life. And when he was present, I got the sense he couldn't wait to be anywhere else. I mourned the virtual loss of my father years ago. The scars had healed and were no longer prominent. All that remained was a dull, flat impression.

My attention shifted to the screen. The game was all tied up in the fourth quarter. Normally a basketball game was only good for background noise, but as the owner, the experience was now different. With less than a minute on the clock, the Knicks possession was intercepted by McCabe and he was now racing up the court. McCabe passed the ball to Pratt and when he couldn't get off a shot, Pratt passed it back to McCabe, who launched the ball from the three-point range. The ball circled the rim before falling in.

I jumped from my chair and released a loud scream. "Yeah baby. That's how you do that shit." I received some hateful stares, but I didn't care. The Ramblers just won 115 to 112. The camera focused on Justus who shook the other coach's hand before the camera angle changed.

"Sit down," Tracie demanded. "Are you trying to get us kicked out?"

"Sorry. But did you see that shit?"

"I saw it. And now I owe Manny fifty dollars on Monday."

"That's what you get for not believing in the Ramblers Way."

"If I didn't know better, I'd think you were actually enjoying these games."

"If the Ramblers win it means money. Which equals more people showing up to the games and buying merchandise."

"Careful, you're starting to sound like your father."

With a roll of my eyes, I ignored Tracie's words. Just because I enjoyed watching one game did not mean I was morphing into a money-hungry capitalist.

Reaching for my phone, I texted Justus.

> Sariah: Congratulations Coach.

To my surprise he texted back immediately.

> Justus: Thank you. Wish you were here to celebrate.

MY PRIVATE JET LANDED IN MCCARRAN AIRPORT AT TEN IN the morning and Mr. Charles was there to pick me up curbside. I was more than capable of driving myself around the city, but Mr. Charles had been my father's driver for years and I had no intentions of leaving him jobless. So he would remain on the payroll and transport me to meetings and back.

At my suite, I took a shower before falling asleep on the couch, still in my robe. When I awoke hours later, my stomach reminded me I'd only eaten a light breakfast on the flight. I shuffled to the kitchen trying to decide whether to cook or order in. My phone dinged from my robe pocket. The screen indicated there was a text message from Justus Chappel. I couldn't help but smile at the sight of his name.

Justus: Are you hungry?

For you? Yes, I thought.

Sariah: I was actually in the kitchen trying to figure out what to eat.

Justus: Get dressed. I'll pick you up in thirty minutes.

Sariah: Okay.

He didn't need to tell me twice. If Justus wanted to see me, I was more than willing to make myself available. I liked a man who took charge. All too often men suffered from indecision, always looking for input. Don't get me wrong, that's fine. But there was just something about a man leading and setting the tone that I appreciated. Making decisions was required of me every day. It was nice to have someone else in the pilot's chair.

True to his word, Justus arrived promptly and we were now traveling west with the top down on his BMW. I was glad I'd opted for a ponytail because my hair was floating on the wind along with the skirt of my dress. My hand on my thigh was the only thing preventing me from flashing my underwear. Late afternoon was transitioning into evening and it felt exactly how a Sunday should. Cruising down Lake Mead Boulevard with Musiq Soulchild serenading us in the background. I couldn't take my eyes off Justus. He seemed so relaxed in his casual button-up shirt, jeans, and sunglasses to protect his eyes from the waning sun.

"Where are we headed?" I asked.

"Have you ever been to a wing tasting?"

"Did you say wine tasting?" It was difficult to hear him over the music and wind whooshing past my ears.

"No, wing tasting, lemon pepper, Louisiana rub, BBQ, Thai chili. The event is held in Morris Park with a bunch of wing masters battling for dominance. We get to rate the best wings of the night."

"Sounds yummy." I scanned his body language, the way his fingers casually tapped the steering wheel to the music. His head nodding in time with the beat. The content smile that settled on his face from the moment he greeted me at my door. "Is this a date?"

Justus slowed at the stoplight and locked eyes with me. "Yes. Is that okay?"

I vigorously nodded my head in the affirmative.

Morris Park was packed. There was a beer garden and a sweet treat suite. I also noted tons of photo worthy opportunities. The aroma of spices, both savory and sweet wafted through the air. My mouth watered in anticipation of the wings I was about to devour. The DJ had a mix of neo soul vibes which I adored. Justus reached for my hand as we passed through a crowd of people so we wouldn't be separated. When the crowd grew less dense, he still held my hand firmly in his.

"How was New York?"

"Busy. Not really much of a break. I had a lot of work to catch up on. But it was nice to sleep in my own bed."

"Have you started looking for a more permanent situation in Vegas?" He pointed toward the beer garden leading us in that direction.

"I'm happy with my current situation."

"Sure you are, but eventually jet setting from coast to coast is going to get old."

"You think I should move to Vegas?"

He ordered our beers and slipped a tip in the jar before handing me one. An Irish red ale with a malty flavor accentuated with a caramel sweetness. It was delicious and I downed several sips in quick succession.

We moved over to an empty high table, sans chairs. "I think you should have a place of residence in Vegas. It doesn't have to be your primary home. But having a residence demonstrates you're invested for the long run."

"Demonstrates to whom?"

"The organization."

I levied a glare in his direction. "You know the NBA reminds me of a cult. Nothing comes before the team, and even family plays second fiddle to the sport and winning."

Justus's broad shoulders hopped. "Not everyone feels like that."

"My father sure did. If Benji or I had an event and it conflicted with a home game, we were shit out of luck because our father would not be in attendance."

"Benji's your brother?"

"Yes." I didn't want to answer any questions about my brother, so I posed a question of my own. "How do you balance it all with your two girls?"

"It's not easy but I've set strict boundaries. I have to be there for every Ramblers game because I'm the coach. But when it comes to all that other extracurricular organizational shit, my twins and their needs take precedence. If one of my girls has an event or if they just need their dad at home for movie night then that is where my loyalty lies. These next few years are going to fly by and I want to be there to experience as much of it as I can with them before they're off to college."

"Sounds like they're lucky to have you." My chest seized a bit like my rib cage was shrinking. What I experienced with my father was very different.

"Being there for my kids is the bare minimum."

I pressed my hand to my tightening chest.

"Are you okay?"

"Yes … no. What you just said was like a gut punch because my father could never find the time. He made himself available for some of Benji's wrestling matches but he always had an excuse for why he couldn't come to my track meets or science stuff."

"And the realization your father made more excuses than actual time for you hurts."

Clearing my throat, I realized this topic was far too heavy for a date. I did not want to talk about my relationship with my father and I didn't want to continue to endure the searing pain which threatened to suck the oxygen from my lungs. "Where are the wings? I was promised wing tasting. It's time to pay up."

Justus allowed me to pivot, reaching for me, he brushed my cheek. "Okay let's get you some wings."

His hand dropped to the small of my back and he guided me forward.

We worked our way through the line of the tasting station. At the front of the line, we are rewarded with a flight of five wings, a scorecard, and a tiny pencil. As we walked to find a table, a man was selling ghost pepper wings touting them as the hottest wings ever. Justus was pulled in by the claim and ordered two servings, which consisted of two wings and two small cartons of milk. We find vacant seating on a long picnic table and settle in.

"I think we should try the sampler first. Because the ghost pepper wing will probably ruin our palates," he said.

"Sounds like a solid plan." I read the scorecard. "First up is the garlic parmesan wing."

The first wing was delicious and I knew this was going to be a tough competition. I moaned as I chewed on the salty cheesy bite. "So good," I said, shielding my mouth with my hand.

Justus nodded in agreement.

After indulging in the wings, we rated each one. Justus gave the Thai chili wing five stars. For me, the superior wing was the apricot sriracha wing. That wing was drool inducing.

"I enjoyed the game Friday night. Tell me what it feels like to win a game?" I used a wet wipe to remove the sauce from my fingers.

"As a coach or as a player?"

"Is it different?"

"Very different."

"As a player."

"When I was a player, I walked into each game with the expectation I was going to win. It was the other team's job to prove me wrong. I'd set foot on that court and it was like a switch would flip. Nothing else mattered. Not the disagreement I may have had with my teammate. Or my wife stressing me out about a new car or bigger house. It was me and the game for four quarters."

"Do you hear the crowd?"

"You hear them but it's muffled. I'm listening to the feet squeaking on the hardtop, telling me my teammate is in position. I'm focused on the defender on the opposing team. Is he going to fake left and then blast right? At the start of the game you want to set the tone quickly and get some points on the board. Every possession matters. When the clock ticks down and you can smell victory in your grasp, you still don't let up. It's not over until the final buzzer blares.

"When we won there was a mix of emotions. I was relieved and elated. My adrenaline, which had been spiking the entire game, finally started to level out. It's like Earth was on pause for four quarters and after the buzzer it resumed its normal rotation."

"And as a coach?"

"As a coach you are acutely aware of everything. Because it all matters. Coaches have to see the big picture. You have to anticipate what could happen four possessions from now and craft a solution to every possible problem. You have to make sure the team is playing well collectively and as individuals. You need to address the weak links because every player has off days and underperforms. I listen to the crowd and their reaction. That's always a great indication of how the game is going.

"When you win it's great but it's more about ticking off a box because you have to repeat that same magic every game for months. Now when you win a big game. Games that if you lose means it's a season ender. When you win those games it's like a … like a good nut."

My eyes grew wide at his unexpected analogy.

"Pardon my language. But there is really no other way to describe the feeling of having all that tension and pressure release in a positive way."

"I have to admit watching the game and your team pull off a win was very exhilarating. I yelled at the TV in a packed bar in lower Manhattan. So you know I was invested."

"Get the fuck out of here," he said, with a horrible New York accent.

"I shit you not. In a room filled with Knicks fans."

"You know you should probably attend a Ramblers game in person."

"I do have a fancy skybox I've never used."

"I would suggest floor seats because that is truly the only way to experience the game."

"I'll see if my assistant can snag me some tickets."

"Are you serious?"

"Yeah, I know tickets go fast."

"You're the owner, I think they'll make exceptions for you." He chuckled. "Are you ready to tackle this ghost pepper wing?"

"No, but I ain't no punk."

He slid the wings in front of us. "On three. One, two, three."

We both bit into our wing. I chewed and waited for the effects to kick in. "It's not very hot," I offered.

Justus remained silent, reaching for his carton of milk.

I coughed as the spice hit the back of my throat and my eyes began to water. My feet tapped under the table and the roof of my mouth burned from the immense heat. "It's too hot," I spit out.

"Here, drink the milk." He offered his carton to me.

I drank between sniffles and tears, which were now rolling down my cheeks. "How are you not dying?" I asked between sips that I swished around my mouth before swallowing.

"My parents are from the Caribbean. They dipped the nipples of my bottles in hot pepper sauce when I was a baby."

Slowly the milk helped to soothe my mouth. It was still noticeably hot, but it was tolerable. "My lips feel singed." I pouted.

Justus stood, rounding the table to sit next to me. Leaning in, he blew on my mouth in an attempt to soothe my charred pucker.

"Is that better?" His brown eyes were fixated on my lips.

"A little." I tugged on his shirt, wanting him to move closer.

Justus licked the corners of my tender mouth before pressing our lips together. When his tongue slipped past, I was gone. Wrapping my arms around him, I slid closer until I was practically in his lap. I didn't care that the park was packed with people and there was a family of four seated directly next to us.

The night air was warm and Justus's kisses were hotter than that ghost pepper wing. After kissing this man, I would need to bathe in a tub filled with milk to cool my core. Justus ignited the fuse buried deep inside. I could feel my lady parts actively excited to receive him. His hand fell to my thigh, inching upward.

"Ahem," the woman next to us said several times before we noticed.

Justus released me and adjusted his shirt to conceal the visible bulge in his jeans. I accepted that although I was ready to hike up my dress and get to hunching face down on this picnic table, we were still surrounded by a crowd.

"Take me home," I practically purred.

JUSTUS

Sariah was stroking my dick and whispering naughty shit in my ear. When I asked her to dinner, I had no expectations the night would turn sexual. I mean I was hopeful, but I would have been content with the conversation, flirting, and maybe a goodnight kiss. My goal was to test the potential of what could be. The last time we kissed it was frantic and spontaneous and I wasn't sure if it was the wine or our pure attraction that was driving us. Maybe it was a mixture of both.

Sariah sat behind me on the couch in just her panties. I leaned back against her bare skin, her pert nipples rubbing against my back. Her legs were sprawled out around me and her hand was massaging my dick. The sight of her beautifully manicured fingers sliding up and down my member held me in a trance. Resting my head on her shoulder, I licked her neck.

"That feels really good," I said between kisses.

"*You* feel really good."

Her hands were slick from the spit, and the friction from the up and down motion made my heart accelerate. I rubbed her bare leg. Sariah's skin was soft and the smell of her was dizzying. She leaned in, kissing my lips slowly, sensually. The pad of her tongue dancing over mine. Her free hand rested on my chest and she manipulated my nipples until they hardened. I in turn thanked her with my heavy breathing and moans.

She dropped her other hand and they worked in tandem to fuck my dick. Her hips grinding behind me like she was practicing for the main event. This woman knew exactly what she was doing. The glint in her eyes as I slowly unraveled was damn near bewitching. Her hand work was slow and methodical with focused attention on the tip. There was this one protruding vein and her finger homed in, rubbing gently as my breathing became erratic. A woman who paid attention to detail was always appreciated, and I planned to reward her with deep thrusts and clit sucks.

I found my feet and reached back to pull her upward. "Sit on my face." Lowering myself into the prone position, Sariah straddled my head. Her hands finding my dick followed by her mouth. Sixty-nine was the perfect position because her pretty lips were now wrapped around me and I could feast on her fat clit.

I cradled her ass, pressing her pussy lips closer to mine. Her slick center turned me on. This woman was hot and ready and I liked to think it was because of me. The fact that she wanted this as much as I did was the ultimate turn on. I focused on her clit and she removed my dick, moaning loudly.

I slapped her ass with a warning. "Put my dick back in."

To my surprise Sariah didn't object she only nodded

before her head sank down reclaiming me. I loved the sound of the slurpy, sloppy head she was offering. Her hips floated over my face looking for a better angle. Following her cues, I repositioned my tongue.

"Fuck," she groaned. Letting me know she appreciated me hitting her spot.

Her tongue swirled around my tip as saliva dripped down my shaft. She fondled my balls before dipping lower and giving them the attention they deserved. Despite Sariah's pussy owning my mouth, the moan that escaped my body was audible. I slapped her ass once again letting her know how good it felt. How good she felt.

Her thighs tightened around my head. Stretching my hand over her silky skin, I pinched her nipples in hopes of heightening her orgasm. Sariah moaned, still rocking over my tongue even while her legs shook and her posture faltered. When she finally regained her breath, she sucked and teased my dick until it exploded. My ears were ringing and my toes were twisted as my pleasure was released. I panted as she swallowed me down with eager enthusiasm.

Sariah licked my member clean before sitting up. "That was …"

"Yeah." I panted trying to catch my breath.

She looked over to me and her eyes were still clouded with desire. Sariah was ready for round two. I on the other hand was still in the preheat stage of arousal. Reaching for the water bottle, I took a sip before handing it to her.

"Do you have any superstitions?" she blurted out.

"Okay, random." I bumped my shoulder into hers.

"Well I'd much rather be screaming your name right now. But since we've paused the action I thought I'd make conversation."

I clicked my tongue. When I was twenty something I could fuck back-to-back. Now at the ripe old age of forty-four I needed a reset. It wouldn't be for long but was still required. So I decided to entertain her line of questioning. "Not really. I do believe splitting a pole while walking is a mortal sin."

"So you don't have any sports superstitions or quirks?"

"Oh I have a few. On game day I have the exact breakfast no matter where I'm at."

"Why breakfast?"

"Because it's the most important meal of the day."

"What do you eat?"

"Two hard-boiled eggs, two strips of turkey bacon, toast with jam."

"And if you have that meal you're sure to win?"

"It's not an exact science but it helps to set the mood for a successful day."

"How long have you been doing that?" She grabbed a chocolate Kiss from the bowl on the coffee table, popping it into her mouth.

"Since I turned pro."

She nodded her head thoughtfully.

"What? Don't you have superstitions you follow?"

"Sure I do. I don't walk under ladders. I don't swim right after eating. I avoid cracks so I don't break my momma's back." She chuckled and her face lit up.

I leaned in, kissing the side of her torso. "Your body is amazing," I whispered.

"That is high praise from a man whose muscles have muscles." She ran her hand over my bicep. "What part of my body do you like most?"

"Shit, where do I start?" I reached for her foot and massaged it. "Your feet are perfect. I kissed each appendage before sucking her toes into my mouth, eliciting a squeal. As I focused in on her big toe, her breathing became dense. "Does this feel okay?" I asked, while fondling her feet at the same time.

"Yes," she eeked out.

My mouth landed on her baby toes and I devoted all my attention to making Sariah squirm. The melody of her laughter was infectious and I was determined to hear it every chance I got.

Releasing her feet, I continued to catalog her impressive attributes. "Then there's the back of your knees which I learned earlier are ticklish."

"Don't you dare."

"Your ass is a masterpiece." Flipping her over, I bit down on one of her humps before spreading her cheeks and burying my face. Sariah's legs kicked up and she moaned into the couch cushions. Pulling back, I rolled her over to her original position. "I think it goes without saying how I feel about your pretty brown lips." I ran a finger across her slit, moving on.

"Let's talk about that belly button. It's deep and shallow at the same time."

"Okay now you're just pulling shit out of thin air."

I licked my lips as my eyes landed on her C cups. It's

difficult to explain but those titties were grown with a teardrop shape and puffy nipples. I'd spent the last few minutes embedding the image of her twin peaks into my memory bank. Kissing her stomach, I traveled to her breast licking the underside of one before wrapping my mouth around her hard nipples. Sariah's hand slid between her legs.

"Did I tell you you could touch yourself?" I asked.

"I didn't know I needed permission." Her expression was defiant.

"You're not coming tonight unless I make you come."

And just like a boss bitch she grabbed my face and said, "Then make me."

With a wicked smirk I said, "Challenge accepted."

SARIAH

Justus was on the floor in search of the condom in his wallet. I snatched it from him, opened the wrapper, and rolled it over his length before straddling his lap. The way his face contorted while I lowered myself onto his dick was my new favorite visual. When I was fully seated and he was snuggly in place, I timidly rocked my hips around his hard shaft, needing to go slow to adjust to his girth.

Justus's lips collided into mine, our kisses fueled by the excitement of finding someone who was sexually on the same level. Wrapping my arms around him, I worked my hips faster. His intense brown eyes were focused on my flushed face. I had a VIP seat to his growing desire. Witnessing him bite down on his lip and groan with pleasure while drinking me in made me want him even more. The sensation of his naked chest grazing my breast only increased my arousal. Our skin-on-skin contact hardened my nipples and left me wet and gushy.

Standing, Justus braced my weight with his arms and took full control. He guided me over his shaft, slowing our movements so I felt every thrust. I had to hold on for dear life when he changed the tempo, lifting me and pumping at an accelerated pace that caused my breath to hitch. The sounds of our bodies made me blush. It was like this man was fucking me in 5K Dolby digital surround sound.

Justus found his way to the bedroom, with no assistance from me, thrusting between steps. He deposited me onto the bed, positioning me on the edge, he dove right back in. Grabbing my leg, he sucked one of my big toes into his mouth and I melted. Men didn't usually pay much attention to my feet. Maybe because my size nines were far from dainty. But I guess to a man with a size sixteen shoe, mine were small and delicate in comparison. I didn't even know I enjoyed foot play, but the way he sucked me and fucked me simultaneously was pure nirvana.

This man's body was perfection, which made sense he was an athlete and even though he was retired, it was clear he wasn't skipping any days in the gym. When he finally dropped my leg, descended on top of me, and moved his hips like he was performing the butterfly stroke, I lost it. The weight and warmth of him made me come undone.

"Justus … yes … please—"

His face was embedded in my chest, suckling and biting my nipples. "Harder," I begged. He bit down on the side of my breast with forceful pressure. I managed a lopsided smile in appreciation. Grabbing his face, I searched for his mouth. When we connected, the kisses he returned were other worldly. His tongue was lethal and he was now coursing through my veins. I was infected with a craving for his special brand of medicine.

"Slut me out," I begged. When I was horny, I lost my filter and became incapable of holding my tongue. I was the type to call out directions and provide generous praise. Men had delicate egos and it was important that he knew I admired his attention to detail. I also wanted him to know that I wouldn't wilt if he roughed me up a little bit. There was a time to be treated like a princess and a time to be treated like a whore and this was the latter.

Justus was a good listener, maybe it was from all those years of being a team player. Without missing a stroke, he flipped me over so I was ass up and bracing his leg on the bed, he took it all. Every last drop of my sanity and all of my self-control. Each thrust ruined my entire life because I knew this wasn't one and done type of dick. This was the dick you stayed up late for. This was the type of dick that made you run bath water and believe nonsensical lies. This dick would have you hand over the keys to your car and cook five course meals.

"Pop that ass for me," he commanded with a hard spank to my butt cheek.

And I did … slinging my ass back on his long, thick, veiny member like the rent was due. Justus slipped his hand underneath me, caressing my breast and fidgeting with my nipples like he was attempting to adjust the reception. My juicy center drove back and forth over his dick and I couldn't help but whimper from the impact.

Justus slid his hand between my legs and with each

thrust he fingered my clit. "Oh my God … you're not playing fair," I breathed out.

"Who said I was playing?"

I inched toward the headboard. His strokes were far too intense, and I was afraid I was liable to sign over half of my estate if I didn't escape.

"Don't run away from it." His voice was deep and gruff. "You said you wanted this."

I nodded weakly.

"Do you still want it?" His tone was less harsh and laced with concern.

"Yes."

Justus gave me what I wanted with a combination of deep strokes. Long and intense, short quick thrusts, and lunges so profound I could virtually feel him in my chest. My body convulsed and my legs shook as I clawed at the bed sheets. His fingers worked my clit as the first wave came. I was thankful I was face down so he didn't have to witness my eyes twitching before rolling to the back of my head. My mouth hung open as my silent scream morphed into a low, animal-like moan. I literally had to fight back tears, the release was so good.

When Justus shuddered and groaned from behind me, my pussy contracted around him and I experienced an unexpected rush, shaking and moaning all over again.

Justus fell to the bed and screamed, "Fuck." His breathing was shallow as he scrubbed his face.

"Is that a good fuck or a bad fuck?"

"It's a, I'm fucked … fuck."

"Why?" *Please don't say this was a mistake.*

"Because I've found my new favorite addiction." Brushing the hair that had escaped my ponytail from my eyes, he kissed me softly on my shoulder and I knew he was right.

———

MY ASSISTANT SCHEDULED THE LUNCH WITH HARPER FOR Monday afternoon. I wanted to get this meeting out of the way. If I didn't, I would obsess about it for the entire week. *Why did she want to meet with me? And how long would I have to fake the funk in her presence?* I followed the housekeeper to the sunroom. It was bright with large windows that provided a view of the left side of the backyard, which was landscaped with blooms and bushes in the shape of animals. From where I stood, I could make out the perfectly symmetrical maze. I'd only walked through once and quickly lost my bearing and had to be rescued.

"Sariah, I'm so happy you could make it." Harper pulled me into a hug. Hugs weren't my thing. I didn't even hug her when I paid my condolences. My body tensed as her hand rubbed my back. "You look stunning as ever. Is that a cobalt blue? I envy you. You can pull off any color. Please sit." She pointed to the table set for two.

"Nice to see you again. How have you been?"

"I have good days and bad days." Harper unfolded her napkin, placing it across her lap. She was wearing a cream dress which made this feel like a garden party. "How have you been holding up?"

"Fine. Work has kept me really busy."

"I asked the chef to make us a crab kale salad. Real crab of course. It's to die for."

"Sounds delish. So … umm … what have you been up to?"

"Well I've been thinking a lot about what to do next now that I have all this free time. I'm seriously considering becoming a social media influencer. You know the women who style their homes and vlog about travel and show off their outfits of the day."

"Really?"

The chef approached with a basket of bread and two shot glasses filled with mushroom soup.

"Yeah, I think I'd be good at that. I really like talking to people and being social so it's a good fit."

"It can definitely be lucrative."

"It's not about the money. My Grover left me set for life. I don't want anything. But it's a nice hobby. Don't you think so?"

I realized as Harper stared at me for approval, I didn't really know anything about this woman. When she started dating my father, shit moved so fast I didn't even know she existed until I received an engagement party invitation in the mail. Instead of actually making an effort to build a relationship, I chose to make sweeping generalizations about her based on little information. I'm not saying she's not a gold digger but maybe there was genuine affection between my father and her.

"Do you have any family in town?"

"No, most of my family is in Minnesota. When I turned eighteen, I moved to Los Angeles to become a model slash actress. My biggest role was as a person of interest on *Law and Order SVU*." She looked off into the distance and cleared her throat. "I don't even know Johnny that well, he's just my dealer. Now if you're not arresting me, I'm leaving." She smiled brightly, proud of her impromptu performance.

I clapped politely. "That was very good."

"I thought so too. And I just knew I was going to be a big star. But things didn't exactly work out that way. I thought about going home. Getting a job as a dental assistant. But then one night I went to a Lakers game and as you know that's where I met your daddy. And he changed my life."

I sipped on the mushroom soup, savoring the blend of flavors. "You two got married quickly."

"We did. But I think we both just knew. Plus your daddy was older and he didn't want to wait. He wanted to start a family."

"Wait what?" I always assumed Harper got knocked up as a way to sink her claws deeper into my father's pockets.

"Grover always felt badly about his relationship with you. I think he wanted a do over. Hoping he'd get it right this time."

In my thirty-eight years on this floating rock, my father never expressed regret. Not about me or Benji or any of it. I was the child, he was an adult and he pushed me away. And after Benji died it just became worse. The way he looked at me like he'd prefer it if Benji was there in my place. I've spent half of my life knowing he wished I was the one who died. He wasn't looking to be a better father, if that were true he could have extended an olive branch in my direction. My father was hoping for Benji 2.0.

I coughed out a laugh. "Is that what he told you?"

"Is it so shocking to believe your father would share things with me that he couldn't with you?"

"Nothing shocks me about that man. But he was not going to be transparent and admit that he wrote me off a long time ago and he wanted another child because the first one was a disappointment."

Harper's forehead attempted to crease but the Botox prevented it. "Disappointment? Your daddy was so proud of you."

I slammed my hand on the table a whole lot harder than intended causing the water glasses to shake. "I do not want to talk about him."

Just like I was unable to conceal my anger, Harper was unable to hide her surprise. "Fair enough but let me just say—"

"No." I pushed back from the table. "If you invited me here to rewrite history or supply the rose-colored glasses to view my father in a new light, I don't want any parts."

"That's not why I invited you. If you leave now you'll miss out on the crab salad."

She was good with people. Every instinct was telling me to bolt but her unwavering smile and sing-song tone helped to suppress my need to be anywhere but here. I reclaimed my seat and as if on cue, the chef returned with two plates, setting them in front of us. We ate in silence with Harper cheerfully humming between each forkful. After several bites I had to admit she was right.

"This salad is very good."

"I know right." She beamed. "I think the secret is in the vinaigrette."

"You might be right." Taking a long gulp of water, I decided to move this conversation along. "As much as I'm enjoying this salad, I can't help but wonder why you wanted to meet?"

"Ahh, just like your father. He was always saying, 'Harper get to the point. If I need additional details, I'll ask for them.'" Her nervous laughter floated in the air. "Well as I've told you I've had a lot of time to think. And of course my thoughts turn to Zander."

I nodded.

"I don't have any family in town. And truthfully most of my family is questionable. I'll just leave it at that. Zander's eight and he doesn't have any cousins his own age or nieces and nephews."

I stared at her still trying to figure out where this conversation was headed.

"He does have a sister."

"Me?" I pointed at my chest in surprise.

"I think it's important for Zander to get to know you. Grover's gone but I want Zander to have ties to his family. And then there's the cultural stuff. I can instruct him but it may be more impactful coming from someone who looks more like him."

"What exactly are you suggesting I do, teach him African American studies?"

"I was hoping you'd be interested in getting to know your brother. He needs family and community. Especially now."

Had I been a good big sister to Zander? No. Spending time with Zander was like training the person who got the promotion you applied for. My father created his new perfect family and that left no room for me. I didn't want Zander to grow up thinking I didn't care. Of course I cared. It was just complicated. The large age gap, the distance with me living in New York, and me being allergic to children. But none of that was his fault. A child shouldn't be punished because the adults couldn't figure their shit out.

"I don't know anything about children."

"Children are easy to please, Sariah. All they need is pizza, a Wi-Fi connection, and candy."

If I declined, I would regret it. I'd act like I was fine, but late at night when the place was silent and my thoughts were loud, I would hate myself for not attempting to be there for him. I hated myself now for not trying. If Benji was here, he would've embraced Zander with open arms. Benji was easy like that, less prone to hold grudges. I on the other hand was the bone collector. Storing away every wrong doing, misconnection, and grievance. And when the time was right, I threw that shit back in your face.

During my time as Grover Thornton's daughter, I'd gathered a shit ton of bones. And anytime he tried to bridge the divide between us, I would scatter the remains to block his way forward. I remembered how it felt after the loss of Benji, the immense loneliness and guilt. Shit, I was still experiencing that pain even after all these years. Zander was probably trying to cope with the complicated emotions surrounding the passing of our father. The last thing I wanted was for him to go through that process alone like I did with Benjamin. "Okay, sure."

Harper clapped her hands with excitement. "I'll have my assistant reach out to yours so we can set everything up."

My stomach coiled in tight knots. I don't think I fully appreciated what I'd just signed up for.

JUSTUS

I FINALLY BIT THE BULLET AND PAID A VISIT TO THE orthopedic surgeon. Dr. Samuelson ran a private practice in Summerlin. Most of her clients were athletes and high-profile celebrities. I'd done my research. Dr. Samuelson was highly respected and was the surgeon of choice for prominent sports figures still at the height of their careers, partly because of her.

My last surgeon was also highly recommended and while my surgery was a success, my confidence was blown. Getting hurt made me scared and when you play with fear or reservation, you're bound to get hurt again. After reinjuring my knee, I forgo surgery and attempted to manage the pain with physical therapy and medication. But I was terrified of getting addicted to prescription drugs so I learned to just work through the pain.

My pain was at a five or a six most days. I'd trained myself to grin and bear it. When I wasn't paying attention, I walked with a limp because I favored my right knee. Truthfully, I should probably invest in a cane. But the last thing I wanted was to be perceived as weak or incapable of performing my job. Strength was a core value in basketball. Damn near every man on and off the court was an Alpha prototype.

I was a horrible patient, rarely taking the advice of the medical professionals. In my opinion no one knew my body better than me. And I was managing my pain pretty successfully on my own, if I do say so myself. But it was becoming clear that without medical intervention, in the long term, my condition would only deteriorate.

My cell phone dinged with a message from my boss and newly acquired fuck buddy.

> Sariah: I need to see you tonight.

> Justus: I can't I have the girls tonight.

> Sariah: ...

I should've probably left it at that, but I'd be lying if I didn't admit I wanted to see her too. Since our rendezvous, I was on pins and needles. Did she feel the same spark, that even after hours of being apart was still glimmering in my chest? All I could think about was hearing her light, effortless laugh. Staring unapologetically in her direction as she licked at the corners of her full lips. And revealing in her excitement when she talked about anything that wasn't basketball.

> Justus: If you want you could join us for dinner tonight.

> Sariah: I don't want to impose.

Justus: It's not an imposition, it's an invitation. Plus, I can't stop thinking about you and would really like to see you.

Sariah: Are you sure your girls won't mind?

Justus: Mind? They'll love it.

Sariah: Okay.

Justus: 3460 Summer Crest Court at seven o'clock.

Sariah:

The door opened and in walked a petite blonde with a bob and chunky green glasses. "Justus, great to meet you. I'm Dr. Samuelson."

"Nice to finally meet you as well."

Taking a seat, she got right to business. "I reviewed your x-rays. I'm probably not telling you anything you don't already know but your left knee is shot. The cartilage is worn down and it's essentially bone on bone."

"You're correct, no surprise there."

"The loss of cartilage is the primary cause for your pain. I saw on your chart you rated your pain at a six most days and stated several days per month it's at a ten which equates to unbearable."

"That's correct."

"What do you do on those ten level pain days?"

"I curse my existence. Send up a prayer and go about my day. Albeit a little cranky."

"You appear to be in excellent shape and you work out regularly. But I have to tell you no amount of physical activity is going to prevent this knee from getting worse. In a few years you will find that your high pain days are more frequent and difficult to work through. I see you were prescribed pain medications but I don't see any recent refills. Are you taking anything for the pain?"

"I prefer homeopathic methods of pain relief."

"Such as?"

"Natural herbs, acupuncture, heat therapy."

"How's that working out for you Coach Chappel?"

"If it was working, I wouldn't be here." I chuckled.

"I feel fairly confident that surgery would alleviate your pain and restore your quality of life. Nothing is ever guaranteed but you are a strong candidate for knee surgery. I think we're looking at a success rate of ninety-eight percent."

"And if I'm in the two percent and it goes wrong?"

"That's a chance I'm willing to take."

Bitch. Of course she was willing to take the chance, it wasn't her fucking knee. She wouldn't be put to sleep with the possibility she'd never wake up. I wasn't going to agree to surgery because my doctor was feeling the vibes. Get the fuck out of here.

"Well with all due respect Doc I don't know that I can say the same."

"It's normal to be scared."

"I never said I was scared." I was terrified. "I just need to weigh the pros and cons and have a discussion with my family." I'm all for taking risks. But I'm conservative with the chances I take. If I'd learned anything from my time in Vegas it was that eventually everyone's luck runs out.

"I totally understand. I'll have my nurse provide you with the informational packet. If you have any questions feel free to give the office a call and I'll make myself available."

"Thank you."

"Coach, when you make your consideration think about your worst pain day and if you can endure that for the next forty years."

Not going to lie, it was giving high sells pressure tactics. She was basically saying I could remain a tired, broken man that cried himself to sleep when the pain got really bad, or I could let her anointed hands cut me open and make it all better. I wasn't ready to take the bait. When I said I needed to think, I meant it.

YES, I'D INVITED SARIAH TO DINNER AT MY HOUSE. AND now I was running around yelling at my girls to tidy up their rooms before I jumped in the shower. Normally I did not do this. I didn't expose my daughters to a woman I was dating until we'd been together for months. I didn't want my girls thinking I was some type of player who used women and moved on to the next conquest. It was important to me that they know their worth and I modeled that in the way I treated them and the way I loved and respected their mother.

I suggested Sariah come over because what I felt for

her was different. Even though it was new and we had no titles, I could see myself with her long term. Truthfully, I wasn't sure how that would work with her being my boss, but I was down if she was. It wasn't just the sex either. Don't get me wrong, the sex was bomb and drove me to distraction, thinking about it anytime I had a free moment. But it was the woman that had me obsessed. Sariah was like one of those Russian nesting dolls. You'd open her up only to find there was more hidden inside to discover. I wanted to learn everything. While Sariah was studying the Ramblers' organization, I was studying her.

An hour later, she was walking through my door smelling good and looking even better.

"Did you have any trouble finding the place?" I leaned in, kissing her cheek with a deep inhale.

"No, I had my driver bring me."

I raised my hands, impressed. "Alright Boss Lady."

"Where are your girls?" she asked, shaking two gift bags in her hand.

"Ahh, they probably didn't hear the doorbell. I'll go get them."

Sariah grabbed my arm, pulling me back toward her. She kissed me like the thought of being separated for even a few brief minutes was too much to bear. I had to mentally will my dick to remain flaccid.

"Are you sure this is okay?"

"Yes." I squeezed her ass before pulling away.

We moved apart just in time. The chatter between Ebony and Jhené entering the room announced their presence.

"Hello," Ebony said cautiously. She was the protective one. While extremely sensitive, she would bend over backward for her family and friends. A trait that was nice, but I was teaching her that it was okay to say no sometimes and that she didn't have to place others' needs before her own.

"I thought you said your boss was coming to dinner?" Jhené asked.

"Yep, this is my boss Sariah Thornton. Sariah, this is Ebony and Jhené." I placed my hand on each girl's head when making the introduction.

"Oh my God. I know you said they were twins but I cannot tell them apart."

"Yep, my little trouble makers.

"Hey," Jhené said.

"I brought gifts," Sariah announced.

"For us?" Ebony narrowed her eyes.

"Yeah, it's just a gift bag with makeup and skincare goodies." Sariah looked at me. "I hope that's alright. If not I get it. I wasn't allowed to wear makeup until I was sixteen. I can totally take these back."

Ebony and Jhené both craned their necks looking at me. "Please Dad."

"Okay, but you will not leave this house with a full face. Lip gloss and mascara like your mom and I agreed on. Is that clear?"

"Yes," the two said in unison.

Sariah handed over the bags and they ran to the family room to check out their goodies. In the kitchen, I poured Sariah a glass of white wine and pulled out a cutting board.

"You know you're their favorite now, right?"

"I'm normally terrible with kids. So I thought I'd give myself a wee bit of an advantage."

I looked out into the family room at my girls squealing over a very large eyeshadow palette. Before turning my attention back to Sariah. "You look nice."

"Thank you."

She was dressed low key in ripped wide-leg jeans and a T-shirt. Her face was clean and I was able to identify the scattering of tiny moles on her cheek, above her lip, and on her neck. God, I wanted to grab her and kiss her. But I opted for kissing her hand instead. I was a cautious man. Weigh all the odds before making a move. But right now all I could think about was how I was going to make this woman my wife.

"What are we making, Coach?"

Clearing my throat and my thoughts, I said, "A whole chicken that's already in the oven because we want it to be nice and golden brown. With that we are going to make some crispy potatoes and carrots and green beans."

"Damn, so you know how to cook, coach, and fuck?" She mouthed the last word.

"Trifecta."

Sariah reached up, touching my cheek. I could tell she wanted to say something, but she bit her lip, thinking better of it and saying instead, "Put me in Coach. How can I help?"

"You can prep the veggies and I'll cut up the potatoes." I handed her a ruffled apron that was normally donned by one of the twins. With music softly playing, she floated around the kitchen washing, peeling, and chopping vegetables. Occasionally her body would graze up against mine on her way to the sink or refrigerator. God, I missed having a partner to lean on. The twins had me outnumbered. A girlfriend would help even the odds. It's weird how you don't know what you're missing until the possibility of that thing is presented to you in living color. The possibility of Sariah being mine was a tantalizing proposition.

At dinner, the girls were full of questions.

"So I'm confused. If you own Genuine Beauty, how are you my dad's boss?" Jhené asked.

"I own the beauty line and the Ramblers team … organization," Sariah said.

"Oh so you're stupid rich," Ebony chimed in.

"We don't ask guests about their pockets. Come on, you know better."

"Well can we ask how long you two have been dating?" Jhené asked.

Sariah coughed on the mouthful of food.

My eyes narrowed. "That's adult stuff. Personal business."

"But you're our father so you're our business," Jhené countered.

"I mean if we're getting a stepmother, I'd kind of like to know," Ebony added.

Sariah released a nervous chuckle squirming in her chair.

"I want you two to understand that I'm going to remember this. And when you both start dating I'm going to be obnoxious."

"So you are dating?" Jhené asked.

"I thought the chicken was really good. Moist and delicious," Sariah interjected in an attempt to change the conversation.

"Yes, I agree. And let's talk about how the green beans and carrots were seasoned to perfection."

Sariah appeared to blush at the compliment. "Just a really good well-balanced meal."

"What are you doing? Is this how adults flirt?" Ebony asked.

"No, it's them changing the subject," Jhené said.

A whoosh of air escaped my lungs. "It's just that you're asking questions that we don't have answers to. I can tell you I like Ms. Sariah. I like her a lot. If I didn't, she wouldn't be here meeting the two most important people in my life. I hope when you get to know her better you like her just as much as I do. But you're going to have to let Dad and Ms. Sariah figure things out in our own time." I turned to Sariah's stunned expression. "Why do you look so shocked?"

"I just … I didn't know you liked me, liked me."

"Yeah well now you know." I stared at her as her face displayed a hint of a smile.

"Are you two about to kiss?" Ebony sounded alarmed.

I tossed a napkin at Ebony. "Let's have dessert."

After dinner, Sariah and the girls abandoned me to clean the kitchen alone. When I was finished, I found them in Jhené's room making a dance video for social media. The trendy beat played while they performed brief choreographed dance moves between laughter.

"I'm going to steal Ms. Sariah from you guys." I reached for her hand.

They groaned their disapproval.

"Please get ready for bed, lights out by eleven."

As we walked down the hall to the main living space, she asked, "Are they always so energetic?"

"They don't stop. If you weren't here it would be me in there shaking my hips."

"I'd like to see that."

"Is your driver just waiting outside?"

"No, I told him I'd text him when I was ready to leave."

"Text him and let him know you're staying the night.

"I can't, I've already taken up too much of your time."

I tossed a glance back the way we came, making sure my girls weren't eavesdropping.

Guiding her hand to my growing dick, I restated my request. "Text him."

She nodded, jaw open and pulled her phone out of her back pocket. I moved to the alarm system, setting it for the night.

"How long have you lived here?"

"I've been coaching in Vegas for three years, so about that long?"

Her eyebrows mashed together. "Did your girls already live in Vegas or did they move with you?"

I scrubbed my beard. "That's a complicated story."

"We have all night."

I always dreaded this part of the getting to know you type conversations. Most women found it hard to believe that my ex and I were able to maintain a friendship after our romantic relationship ended. We weren't best friends, it was more like a brother-sister dynamic at this point. I know that sounds weird, but over time we moved past the hurt and learned to appreciate the things that made us fall in love in the first place. My ex was an amazing woman and a great catch. She just wasn't for me.

Claiming Sariah's hand, I led her down the hall leading to my bedroom on the other side of the house. "We were all living in North Carolina. I was the assistant coach for the Charlotte Talons. When I got the call from the Ramblers I prayed about it and then I asked my ex-wife to make the move with me."

Sariah's eyes grew wide.

"Platonically, so I could be close to the girls."

"And she said yes? Just up and left her job and family?"

"We didn't have family in North Carolina and she's a makeup artist. She can work from anywhere."

"So you two are still really close."

"She's family." I unclasped my watch, placing it in the drawer dedicated to watches, ties, and cuff links.

Sariah pinned her arms over her chest. Her relaxed body language was now rigid.

"What?" I asked.

"I didn't say anything."

"You didn't have to, your face is doing the communicating for you."

Her shoulders hopped. "I knew something had to be

wrong with you. You were too perfect. Of course you have baby momma drama. Of course."

"There isn't any baby momma drama. We're cool and we co-parent."

"So she moved down here, what, out of the kindness of her heart?"

"She moved because family is important to us. Those girls …" I pointed in the direction of their bedroom. "Are important to us. Ebony and Jhené are the best thing that she and I ever did."

"Justus, I can't. My life is so chaotic right now I can't deal with your drama too."

I closed the space between us, cupping the sides of her face in my hands. "There is no drama. Melody is good people and I love her because she is the mother of my kids. The romantic part of my relationship with her has been over for years. There are no blurred lines or drunken nights of flirting that lead to fucking. I'm single. I do not play games. I say what the fuck I mean and I mean what the fuck I say. Now … I am actively trying to pursue you." Jostling my shoulders, I continued, "But if this isn't what you want then you should leave."

Sariah's facial expression transitioned from annoyance, to shock, to wariness until it settled on longing. Her eyes, once narrow with skepticism, were now tender with possibilities. She heeled off her boots, indicating she intended to stay a while.

"When you texted me earlier you said that you needed me." With the pad of my thumb, I stroked her lips. "Tell me exactly what you need." I slid my thumb into her mouth and she worked her tongue around, sucking and slurping like it was an extension of my dick.

When she paused, she whispered, "I need you to help me forget and remember all at the same time."

"What are you forgetting?"

"All of it. All the expectations."

"And what are you trying to remember?"

"The way I felt when your big dick was snuggly inside me. The way the world seemed to fall away around us." She tugged at my shirt, pulling it from my pants. "I want to escape with you."

"I'll be your refuge. But eventually I hope we can build a life you don't want to run from." I planted a kiss on her neck.

"Is that even possible?"

"With me …yes."

"God, you're so cocky." She pulled my polo over my head. "I love that about you."

I slid her jeans over her curvy thighs. "Ass or pussy?"

"What?"

"Do you want me to eat your ass or pussy first?"

"Wow, I love those options."

"I aim to please."

Grabbing hold of my dick, she lightly stroked it. "Ass."

Being a pussy pleaser was embedded in my DNA. Spreading her ample cheeks, I went to town. First, I teased her until her breath was shaky and she fisted the sheets. When I dipped my tongue inside, Sariah became vocal. Praise was followed by directions and pleas for me not to stop. Her legs were trembling, and she collapsed face first into the mattress in hysterics. Giving her ass a slap, I turned her over.

Sariah was still at the peak of her orgasm and I decided to be a menace and not let up. Dropping to my knees, I claimed her clit. No gentle licks or kisses, just concentrated suction on that fat clit which made her eyes roll to the back of her skull. She was spread eagle, arms over her head. I could tell she was close to coming again and I was lightweight jealous. Lucky her was two to my zero in the orgasm department. I needed to catch up.

My thoughts were interrupted by Sariah pushing my head away while screaming through her second wave. I pulled back with a huge smirk.

Brushing her hair from her face, she stared up at me. "Don't get full of yourself."

"What? I'm just happy I can make you happy."

"You're happy you can drive me crazy. But I have tricks too." She was rubbing her nipples, which made it difficult to concentrate.

"Bring it on then."

Sariah grabbed my arm, pulling me to the bed, and quickly straddled me. When her wet and gushy sweet spot surrounded my dick, I was transported to a space where only this mattered. Sariah, me, and our shared pleasure. She rode my shaft like I stole something, was convicted, and sentenced to twenty-five to life inside her tight pussy. When I reached for her breast, she captured my wrist and held them over my head. Gotdamn I never realized how strong she was. Leaning closer, she teased me, keeping her lips just out of kissing range.

"Don't play with me," I groaned.

"I'm not."

"Then kiss me."

"If you want a kiss, I think you should beg for it." Realistically I could overpower her and take the kisses she owed me, but I was big on consent. It was also important to note that she said this while her hips floated over my dick. I would bark like a seal if she commanded me to.

"Please … I need to feel your body, touch your skin." My voice hitched as she slid down my length. "I want to worship at the altar of Sariah Thornton."

Sariah leaned closer once more and whispered, "Fuck me." Releasing my hands, she pulled back and I pounced. I wrapped my arm around her waist. I pulled myself up and flipped her onto her back. From there, each stroke was backed with intention. Burying my hand in her hair, I fucked her mouth with my tongue. The kisses were rough and messy as we moaned over one another. With my hand on her thigh to pin it open, I swam laps in her pussy. Sariah responded to every stroke and we were like synchronized fuckers working in tandem in pursuit of a much-needed nut.

"See what happens when you play games? You get punished," I said breathlessly.

Sariah's eyes were glassy and unfocused. I loved how undone she became over me. Look, I was no slouch in bed, but Sariah responded like I was the pussy whisperer. Which was fair because I did know exactly what she needed, which in this moment was slow, deliberate thrusts that felt so deep she'd swear I was taking up space in her chest. I fucked her into a united nirvana with me gripping her hips and pouring my soul into her. Sariah rubbed my head absentmindedly until we both floated back down from our high.

Some things I just knew for certain, the Ramblers were on the precipice of a championship in the next few years, the show *Friends* was a total rip off of *Living Single*, and Sariah Thornton was mine. She didn't have to say it. Her heart, soul, and pussy were now in my charge. I just needed to make sure not to fuck it up.

SARIAH

"Can I get one of those foam fingers?" Tracie asked, as we made our way to our courtside seats.

I took Justus's suggestion and decided to attend a Ramblers' home game in person. And since Tracie was in town visiting, I dragged her with me. We were in the front row, center court, right in the thick of the action. I would've preferred the privacy of the skybox, but Justus claimed center-court seating was like being in the heart of the game.

Entering the arena, I was struck by the rumble of conversation and movement as fans settled in. Fans donned red and white, the team colors. We passed several individuals with signs that read Rambler Nation. And one man with his face painted in a checkerboard red and white pattern. It was truly impressive to see all of these people here to watch the Ramblers play.

The teams were already on the court warming up. Tracie and I walked past the Ramblers bench and I stopped to acknowledge the coaching staff. The last thing I wanted was for my presence to be a distraction but I did want to show my support and express my enthusiasm for the game.

Assistant Coach Klay's back snapped to attention when he noticed me approaching. "Hello Ms. Thornton, so happy to have you in the building."

"Thanks Coach Klay and please call me Sariah. I'm very excited and wearing my Ramblers Red." I tugged at my bedazzled sequin jersey with my name on the back and the number one. After introducing Tracie we quickly moved on.

I spotted Justus immediately wearing a tailored suit and serious expression. A ribbon of excitement fluttered inside my tummy. It was safe to proclaim that I was smitten. I tried my best to wrestle the smile that threatened to overtake my features. Justus was engrossed in his clipboard. Moving in his direction, I said, "Hi Coach Chappel." He slowly raised his head but his eyes were unfocused, almost as if he was looking past me. "I just wanted you to meet my friend Tracie."

Justus's head was on a swivel, barely registering Tracie's presence. "Nice to meet you. Enjoy the game." His response was curt as he turned and walked away, flagging down player number twelve to offer instruction.

"Very friendly," Tracie teased.

When we took our seats, I apologized. "He's usually more personable."

"He's probably just preoccupied with preparing for the game."

"Yeah, I'm sure you're right. But it was a touch rude. Like I wasn't expecting him to roll out the red carpet.

But I had hoped he'd be happier to see me … and meet you."

"Babes … you're doing that thing you do when you obsess."

"I just really wanted him to meet my best friend." I tried to make my irritation more about the slight against her and less about me.

I'd been looking forward to seeing him all day. Thinking about the cute wink and nod we'd share when I called him Coach Chappel. The invisible current of electricity that would pass between us while he tried his best to resist the urge to touch me. His eyes backlit by fire with the understanding that later on that evening we would be crashing into one another with gropey hands and eager lips. Our meet up did not live up to the fantasy I'd built in my head. I didn't expect him to bend me at the waist and plant a kiss to my mouth, but a sign he was happy I was there would've gone a long way.

"Look at him, that man is in his zone right now. No room for interruptions," Tracie said.

He did look super hot as he walked across the court to speak to our star player, Colin Pratt. Justus's stride made it clear that Quest Center Arena was his house. I always found confidence sexy and Justus was dripping in it.

"Agreed." I didn't want to be the woman who made her relationship with a man her entire identity. But Justus was a bright spot in my life right now. Being back in Las Vegas I was constantly confronted with the past. The shoulda, woulda, coulda's that made up my life's journey. Justus was unexpected and exciting and the possibility of getting this right … the romantic aspect of my life intrigued me.

I'd never been this close at a sporting event in my life. The last time I witnessed the Ramblers play live I was probably seventeen. My dad took Benji and me to one of the games. I remember him strutting into the underground tunnel all smiles as people approached to meet his children. Oddly enough, I also remember how he gushed over us. Telling staff and colleagues about how I was being recruited by colleges because of my 4.5 GPA and philanthropic activities and that Benji was a starter on his basketball team.

My father told these people things I was surprised he knew. Like the fact that my high school debate team had come in second at the statewide competition. He never showed up to any of my events but the way he was bragging, you would think he was front and center. That visit was also my first time in the skybox and while I wasn't into basketball, I enjoyed the perks of being the owner's daughter. Unlimited food and soda, a bird's-eye view of the court, and televisions everywhere you turned.

When the game started and the Ramblers made their first two points, I had to remind myself to remain seated. The impulse to jump out of my chair like a proud mother was overwhelming. I don't remember the basketball games being this interesting when I was younger, but today I was engrossed. Focused on every turn over, rebound, and free throw. Perhaps it was because of the time I'd been spending with Justus learning about the organization and the game. Or maybe sitting center court as the players hustled past was bringing out the fanatic in me. Justus was correct, watching a sporting event live in real time was way more thrilling than sitting in a cramped bar or on the couch with lukewarm pizza and flat beer.

At one point in the game, power forward Deion McCabe almost crushed Tracie in an attempt to grab a rebound. Tracie reached out to stop his momentum, touching his rock-hard abs. For the next fifteen minutes, I had to listen to her replay the experience with colorful adjectives and added imaginary scenarios.

The game was a nail biter the entire way through. I don't know how Justus could keep up. I was just as invested in the action on the court as I was to Justus's performance on the sidelines. He was barking orders, directing plays, hyping up his players, and at one point had a nasty exchange of words with a ref. Not going to lie, that part turned me on. In the end, the Ramblers squeaked out a win in overtime.

As the players headed to the locker room, I shouted my congratulations. "Good job, so proud, great job." I'm not really sure what I was supposed to say, but I wanted them to know I appreciated their hard work. Justus's steps were brisk, but he did slow his stride long enough to shoot me a look from across the court that weakened my knees. It was a look that said he was going to punish me in the best possible way. The "it's too deep I can't take any more, please don't ever stop fucking me" kind of way. I didn't appreciate being ignored earlier and he was going to have to make it up to me. What could I say? When it came to this man, I was a greedy bitch.

"That was awesome." Tracie jumped up from her seat. "This team is amazing and you own it." She chuckled in disbelief.

"It was fun. Seeing it in person was ten times better than on TV."

"When number twenty-seven almost smothered us with his body weight ..." Tracie made an obscene slurping sound. "That's a beautiful way to die."

Ignoring her words, I asked, "Do you want to go do something? I'm too amped to just head home."

"Do you think you could get me into the locker room?" she teased.

"Absolutely not." My phone chimed in my hand.

Justus: Drinks?

Sariah: Sure.

Justus: Bring Tracie. I'd like to properly introduce myself.

Sariah: We can meet up at the Waldorf and have drinks in the lounge?

Justus: Sounds perfect. I'll meet you there. I have to talk to the press.

Sariah: Okay.

"I know that must be Justus because you are seriously grinning at your phone right now."

I hooked my arm in hers and walked through the arena, headed toward the executive exit where Mr.

Charles was parked out front. "We're meeting Justus for drinks."

"Great, then I can ask him what he did to make you all love sick."

I stopped in my tracks. "Love? Slow your horses there partner. I like him. He's cool. It's nice having someone to fuck when I'm in town." I shrugged.

"It's more than fucking. You light up when you speak about him and you were all butt hurt when he was too busy to talk to us before the game."

"I just enjoy the attention."

"Okay you like the man. You *love* his dick. But let's not pretend you wouldn't be down for more. And it sounds like Coach Chappel is looking to provide."

"I'M SORRY YOU GOT YOUR HEAD STUCK IN WHAT?" JUSTUS asked. His arm was casually slung over the booth behind me.

"It was a vase. And I was drunk," I said.

"What I still don't understand is what possessed you to put a vase over your head in the first place," Tracie added.

"I … was … drunk."

"How did you get it off?" Justus asked.

"We had to break the vase. It ruined everybody's high," Tracie laughed.

"Don't look at me like that." I pouted in his direction.

"I'm just in awe." He brushed a wayward strand of

hair from my face. Usually shit like that happens when you're five, not thirty.

"Let's not act like you've never done anything stupid," I said.

"Spill the beans, mister." Tracie giggled while taking a sip from her glass.

Justus turned his gaze toward the spattering of customers still nursing drinks in the lounge. Apparently, we were the closing shift. Rubbing his beard, he finally spoke. "Okay when I was a player in the off season I would play overseas in Spain. One night I got hammered and me and this beautiful woman headed over to the beach. We're making out and then she pulls out a gun and steals all my shit. My wallet, my sneakers, my watch and necklace, and all my clothes. She left me on the beach butt booty ass naked."

I covered my mouth trying to hide my amusement at his misfortune. "So what did you do?"

"I walked back to the hotel, went to the front desk with my naughty bits covered by my hand and asked for a towel."

"Did they ever catch the thief?" Tracie asked.

"No."

"Just ass cheeks out in the hotel lobby," I said.

"Ass cheeks out and little Justus barely covered."

"That was embarrassing. Thank you for sharing." My bestie smirked.

Justus tipped his glass in Tracie's direction.

I think we all hope our best friend and the guy we fancy will get along. And I was delighted to see the two sharing a laugh. Justus was night and day from the abrupt coach from hours ago. Per usual, Tracie was right, I'd worried for nothing. Maybe I just need to get used to his focused, game day demeanor.

After another hour of stories, Tracie headed to her room and Justus and I made our way to my suite. Heeling off my shoes, tonight's win was still at the forefront of my mind. "It was a good game. You should be proud."

"It was too close. We made stupid mistakes and turn overs. We're lucky we won because we did not deserve it the way we were playing." Justus pulled his loosened tie from his neck.

"I thought a win was a win."

"Technically, but the team we played against was weaker and we should've dominated them. Instead we got our asses handed to us for much of the game."

"How do we fix that?"

"Honestly, we need a young, hungry, solid player."

"We have Colin Pratt."

Justus smirked. "Colin is thirty-five. He's a great player don't get me wrong. But he is at the very end of his prime playing years. Couple that with his arrogance and he's a problem."

"What are you saying?" My father spent years rebuilding this team. When I came to visit, he always insisted on taking me to dinner and he would talk ad nauseam about all the plans the organization was implementing to get the team back to playoff contenders. I only half listened, but I did remember the acquisition of Colin Pratt being a big part of that.

"I'm saying we don't have a winning team. Can we

make it to the playoffs? Yeah sure. Can we make it to the finals? Not a stone's throw chance in hell." Justus removed his shoes and suit jacket. "Do you want to smoke?"

"Yes." I followed him to my wraparound balcony.

This time he had a traditional wrapped blunt. He used my candle lighter to light the tip and took a long drag before handing it to me.

After a few passes back and forth, I asked. "So what do I do to fix the Colin problem?"

"We need to be actively recruiting his replacement now. Same with Deion McCabe. Deck's a great player he hustles on that court but he is older than Colin and when his contract ends I don't think he'll want to re-up and I know the Ramblers will want to break ties." He blew out a cloud of smoke. "Unless you have other thoughts?"

I didn't have any thoughts. I'd never given the player roster much consideration. It seemed like it was working, so why fix it? But Justus was right, the Ramblers hadn't been in the finals in over seven years. And last year was the first time we'd made it into the playoffs in a long time. The team functioned but they weren't a premier league.

"Maybe I should talk to Nolan and see what he thinks."

Justus pulled his face into a pained expression. "Umm … Nolan isn't the boss, you are."

"I know. But I just need advice."

"I wouldn't look for advice from Nolan."

"But he's my GM, he's supposed to have my back."

I'd known Nolan for years. He was my father's closest advisor and he was ever present at holidays and special events. So when I took over ownership, he welcomed me with open arms. He'd offered on more than one occasion to answer any and all questions, and he claimed he was here to support me in this transition. For the most part, I believed him, but I couldn't shake the nagging feeling that I should remain cautious because his assistance was bound to come with strings.

Justus leaned forward in his oversized chair. "Do you feel like he has your back, Sariah?"

"I don't know. I don't fucking know. This shit was thrown in my lap and people expect me to make these big sweeping decisions about the future of the organization and players' careers. Not to mention this isn't the only business I inherited. I have a portfolio of assets all demanding my attention. And then there's Genuine Beauty, my company, my heart and I'm forced to put it on a side burner. I don't know why my dad did this but I know it was to hurt me."

Unloading on Justus wasn't fair, but I was exhausted from the unrelenting weight of my responsibilities. So many people were counting on me to get it right. My fear of burning everything down was a road block keeping me frozen in indecisiveness.

"You could always sell."

"Is that what you think I should do?" I examined his face, looking for answers.

"I think you need to come to a decision on your own."

I rested my hands on Justus's folded arms. "I trust you. So tell me what to do."

"That's not how this works. Baby, I get that you're overwhelmed. I understand overseeing a sports team is new to you. And I can't imagine having to deal with the Ramblers while also making decisions about the other companies that have fallen into your lap. But one thing I've learned during our brief time together is that you are more than capable of running this team … if that's what you want."

I never intended for our night to end like this. And I was in no way prepared to make life-changing choices tonight. "Can we talk about something else? Do something else?" I didn't even have the strength to artfully switch the subject.

"Sure what do you want to talk about?"

My eyes transitioned to lascivious as they tripped down his body. I was trying to lose a few hours locked in his embrace. "I want you to talk me through it. Tell me how good I feel. And ask me if I like it." The corners of my mouth contorted into a devious grin. "I want you to tell me what drives you crazy and how you can't wait to come. And then I want to drop to my knees and slurp up every single drop."

Justus stood, towering over me. He cupped my neck in his massive hand. His thumb stroked the side of my neck. "Are you going to be a good girl?"

"Yes."

"Are you going to listen to everything I say?"

"Yes." I let go of a nervous giggle, uncertain about what I'd gotten myself into.

"First, I'm going to need you to strip. I want to look at you." Releasing me, he dropped back into his chair and took slow drags from the blunt.

Shimmying out of my clothes as seductively as possible, I witnessed his dick pressing against his pants. The slight chill in the air mixed with the fact I was stark naked on a semi private balcony fifty-seven stories in the air was titillating.

"Are you wet for me?"

I hiked my leg onto the armrest of his chair and inserted two fingers inside my pussy. Plunging them in and out so he could ogle just how much I wanted him. When I was done Justus claimed my hand, licking my fingers clean.

Jumping to his feet, he led me to the balcony railing. "Eyes forward."

I obeyed in silence, gazing over the cityscape. The rustling behind me elicited shudders down my spine as I waited not so patiently for Justus to overtake me. Not knowing what he was doing or when to anticipate his touch was a torturous pleasure. When he finally grasped my waist, my hands gripped the railing to brace myself. Justus wasted no time hooking his arm underneath my leg so he could easily slide inside.

Expertly working his length into my depth, he spoke low and soft so I had to focus to hear him. "You're doing so well letting me stretch you out. Can you feel how hard I am for you?"

He was in so deep he was stealing my air. All I could muster was a weak gasp.

"Don't be rude. I asked you a question." He was using each thrust as a tool to coerce words from my lips.

My throat was dry, but I managed to reply. "Yes, you're so hard."

"Keep it up, just like that."

I wrapped my arm over his shoulder. My body and all he was doing to it was on display to anyone with a zoom feature on their phone. Getting fucked was my only concern. And Justus was capable of fucking me until I was squirting juices down my thighs and all over his dick. With the one foot that was still touching the ground, I did my best to meet each stroke.

Justus took note and dropping my leg, he slapped my ass spurring me along. Clutching the railing, I steadied myself and reared my ass over his shaft until my legs wobbled and my throat was hoarse from screams of pleasure. His hand swept over my breast and came to rest as his fingers palmed my nipples. The already taut tips pebbling into hard nibs.

"Let's reward this effort." His hand traveled down my torso and landed on my core. His nimble fingers located my clit and fucked me like a maestro directing a concert. Each thrust perfectly timed with a flick of his thumb. The pacing of his strokes aligned with the rotation of his fingers working in small circles forcing me to cry out.

"Are you ready to come?" he asked.

Was there any other option? He'd had me tittering along the edge of pleasure and release for twenty minutes. Part of me never wanted the warmth of his body pressed against mine to end and the other part wanted all the joy that letting go would bring.

"Yes." My teeth were chattering.

Without warning, he lowered me to the chaise and fucked me until I dissolved. Awash in an otherworldly pleasure. Justus brushed the hair from my face and assured me, "You're doing good. You're doing so good." My eyes rolled to the back of my head and my body shook violently as the orgasmic wave took form.

When my eyes finally focused, Justus was looking down at me, his face lit by the afterglow. "I can never get enough of you."

JUSTUS

"THAT'S IT, YOU GOT IT. JUST TWO MORE," DECK encouraged me.

I pushed the weighted bar upward with a labored breath.

"One more and you're golden."

I grunted through the last set. It wasn't pretty but it was done.

"Good job." Deck swatted me on the knee.

Lowering the weights to the resting position, I stood shaking out my sore arms. "Let me ask you something."

"Shoot," Deck said, searching for heavier weights so he could out lift me.

"What do you think of Aldridge Mosley?"

He expelled a breath of air. "First-round draft pick, leads in scoring, league MVP. He's a good all-around player. Kids got a bright future ahead of him."

"What if that future included the Ramblers?"

"A player like Mosley ain't coming to the Ramblers."

"Don't be so sure. We have a lot to offer. Right now he's playing in the boondocks. He could be in Las Vegas. What is he, twenty-five or twenty-six? Perhaps he's considering a move to warmer weather where there're parties, entertainment, and people who look more like him."

"Maybe, but at the end of the day he has to want to play on this team."

"And we will compensate him handsomely for doing so."

"What about Colin?"

I flashed Deck a dubious look. Colin and him were friendly, but he knew as well as anyone that Colin Pratt's expiration date was fast approaching.

Deck continued, "Colin likes being the star, he will not settle for sharing the spotlight."

"He'll get used to it," I said, adjusting my lifting glove.

"Wait, you're sounding like this is something the organization is actively pursuing."

I wasn't in a position to confirm or deny but I was seriously considering the possibility. And I just so happened to have the ear of the owner who respected my opinion. If she intended to keep this team, I wanted to help her be successful and adding Moseley to our lineup would almost ensure that. "The Ramblers aren't pursuing shit but I'm just weighing options. I gotta stay ready so I never have to get ready."

"You know who else is getting ready?"

"Who?"

"Busch. He was sniffing around after practice the other day. Pulled me aside and asked me all sorts of questions about Sariah."

"Oh yeah? Like what?" I re-tied the string of my shorts, hoping I didn't come off too eager.

"General questions about how I liked her as an owner. Personal questions about whether she was sleeping with anyone on the team."

My eyebrows hiked up my forehead. Desperation was making Nolan bold. "What did you say?"

"I didn't say shit. I don't know her like that. And I was certainly not going to rat you out."

"Rat *me* out?"

"Come on dude. You two are fucking or you're on the precipice of fucking."

"She's my boss."

"Yeah and there ain't nothing in the rules and regulations about sleeping with team owners so you're good. But I don't think Busch needs to know your business."

I scanned the gym to confirm we were alone. "Is it really that obvious?" I worked my jaw into a tight circle.

"No. But I know you and anytime that woman enters a room you only have eyes for her. And on the off chance you're not looking at her she is mad dogging you. So clearly you are laying some deep pipe."

Sariah and I had an unspoken agreement that it was best to keep our relationship on the low. She was in a delicate position as the new owner, and the last thing she needed was the stigma that would naturally come from dating me. And I could do without people thinking the only reason I remained on payroll was because I was diddling the boss.

Since Deck was my closest friend, I nixed my no comment rule and allowed myself to rave for a minute.

"She's so fucking amazing." Having the opportunity to finally talk about my budding relationship with Sariah was a relief. When you're falling for someone, you want to shout it from the rooftops and share your joy. "She's confident in her skin and the conversations are effortless. It's just cool vibes whenever we're together. And she is sexy as fuck." Just the thought of her made my dick jump.

"She's stunning, I can't even lie."

"The fact that a woman like her doesn't have a man is insane."

"Wait, aren't you, her man?"

A glaze settled over my eyes. "I …"

"Whoa. So you just have her out here in these streets as a free agent? Available to jump on any dick she pleases."

"We haven't talked about titles. But trust me she is invested. If you know what I mean." I offered a cocky chuckle.

"She may be invested but she ain't taken. That means it's open season. And the way eyes were locked on her when she showed up to the game the other night, you have competition."

"Pfst … listen I'm not territorial in the least but if you ask her who it belongs to, she will tell you Justus Aloysius Chappel." I patted my chest for emphasis.

"Aloysius?" Deck screwed up his features. "Your momma and daddy named you Aloysius? How am I just now learning about this? Are you one of those fantastical negroes?"

"First, shut up. And second, we don't need titles when we know exactly what time it is."

"Well whatever you do. Don't ever tell her your middle name because it is difficult to get wet for a dude named Aloysius," Deck teased.

"Yeah, well all of our middle names can't be Diesel like you."

"DDM baby." He pretended to shoot an imaginary ball.

———

GENERAL MANAGER BUSCH INVITED ME TO AN IMPROMPTU lunch. He said he was meeting with someone very important and wanted me there. It wasn't unusual to participate in meetings or events, especially when the organization wanted to make a good impression. As coach, I was considered the face of the team when the star players were unavailable.

I showed up to Nobu early and found Nolan Busch already enjoying a drink.

"Ahh Justus … my boy." He gave me a stiff pat on the shoulder.

My jaw clenched. I was a grown ass man and I was certainly no one's boy. But Busch was a condescending prick. And while basketball was a predominately Black sport, the faces in upper management were less so. Unfortunately for me and many others in the league, we were forced to grin and bear micro-aggressions and often-times blatant racism if we wanted to hold on to our jobs.

"How have you been?" I asked, unbuttoning my suit jacket before taking a seat.

"Margaret is trying to convince me to fund my son's gap year. And I opened my portfolio to find my youngest had drawn all over my important documents."

"Gap year?"

"Yeah, he wants to travel the world and fuck random women. When I was his age, I was working in my father's company learning the business before heading off to college. The kids today are a different breed. Luckily for you, you have girls. All you have to worry about is making sure they marry someone who can take care of them so you no longer have to foot the bill." He took a sip of his dark liquor.

"Well I'm hopeful my girls will go off to college and pursue careers that make them happy. Marriage can definitely wait."

"Hmm, you say that now but when they're begging for money at twenty-five you may feel differently."

I shook my head in a swift arch. Nolan was the last person I'd take parenting advice from. His kids stayed in some type of trouble. The latest being a fraternity hazing scandal involving his oldest who was a senior in college.

"You only have the two, right?" Nolan asked.

"Yes."

"Well take it from me, don't have any more. I'm sixty-three with a six-year-old. A bratty defiant six-year-old." He looked at his documents damaged by green and orange crayon.

I ordered seltzer water. Unlike Busch it was too early to indulge in hard liquor.

"Who are we meeting with?" I asked.

"Derek Wayne. He was in town for a quick trip and I convinced him to make some time to meet with me. As the coach I wanted you here to show we are serious in our desire to make the organization as successful as possible."

Clutching my glass, I took a long silent drink. It would appear Busch was still seriously pursuing new ownership. I wasn't exactly sure what the game plan was. Sariah was a majority owner with sixty-five percent of the shares. The remaining thirty-five percent was spread between a dozen or so individuals and groups. As majority owner, what Sariah said goes. It wasn't as simple as voting her out, because she had the lion's share of the voting power.

"Speak of the devil and he will appear," Nolan said when he caught sight of Derek.

Derek Wayne was imposing. I was tall, but even I had to crane my neck to look at him. He was a legend and his games were some of my favorites to rewatch. Wayne was now well into his fifties but he was an athlete who appeared to have succeeded in retirement, making more money now than when he was on the court. He was dressed in a tracksuit. His casual style was kind of what he was known for. A business man that didn't have to don the monkey suit to succeed.

Nolan stood, arm outstretched to greet Derek. The restaurant patron's attention shifted to our table. Derek

Wayne was a celebrity and when he walked into a room, it didn't go unnoticed.

"Nolan it's good to see you again." Derek's voice was a rumble.

"Derek, you remember Coach Chappel."

"Yes, Justus and I have met several times." His hand shake was like a vise.

"It's good to see you again," I said.

We settled into our seats. Derek ordered a drink and we placed our food orders. The conversation began innocuously enough. How are the wife and kids? What are your plans for the summer? Did you catch the Warriors game last night? By the time the food arrived, the conversation shifted.

"Coach Chappel, what are your thoughts on your new owner?" Derek asked, cutting into his steak.

"She seems to be making a concerted effort to get to know the team," I said.

"Busch says she doesn't know the first thing about the NBA or what it takes to oversee an organization like the Ramblers."

"Sariah Thornton is a successful business owner. It would be wise not to underestimate her." My lips pressed into a fine line.

Nolan waved my words aside. "She doesn't even like basketball."

"I beg to differ." Rancor burned through my veins. "Sariah sat courtside at a recent game and was invested. She was yelling and encouraging the team. I don't know but she appeared to be enjoying herself."

I was trying to walk a fine line. It was important

Nolan and Derek believed I was open-minded and willing to hear their perspective, but I wasn't going to let them dog pile on Sariah. She may not be my girlfriend, but an attack on her felt like an attack on me.

Derek raised his hand, shaking the remaining ice in his glass in search of a refill. "The game will do that to you. Even a newbie like Sariah can't help but get excited."

"Excited or not, she's beyond her depth. I'm still scratching my head as to why Grover chose to leave the Ramblers to her," Nolan grunted.

"Maybe her father trusted she could get the job done," I offered.

Nolan and Derek laughed like they were at an open mic night and I was the featured comedian.

"She doesn't even know what the NBA stands for," Nolan challenged.

My face folded into a frown. I was shocked too a few weeks ago when her answer was the National Basketball Assembly. But I can guarantee you she would never get that shit wrong again after I made her study the acronyms for a week and tested her on them.

"Is there a learning curve? Sure," I said. "But she is learning."

Nolan tossed his linen napkin on his plate. "This sport doesn't offer on-the-job training. As owner you need to be ready to hit the ground running. Produce or perish."

"I guess I'm just not understanding how you intended to get Sariah to sell. As the majority owner she can't be voted out. There is no board to answer to. She's not just going to let you take her shit."

"That's where I come in," Nolan said. "I've been slowly building her trust and she relies on me for advice."

"So you're going to advise her to sell?" I asked.

"You're damn right and I'm going to make her think it was her decision."

"Once we get Sariah out of the way we can focus on the organizational goals. Acquiring new players and building a championship team," Derek added.

"And if you were in our camp on this ... well that kind of loyalty is invaluable." Nolan rubbed his thumb and index fingers together. "Extended contract, signing bonus, executive corner office. You'd just have to name your price."

The two of them sounded like villains in a B movie. All that was missing was the swirly mustaches and the dastardly laughs. I'd like to think Sariah would fight to retain control of the team, but the way she was talking the other night, it sounded like Nolan may be actually wearing her down. She almost seemed defeated. Whatever she wanted to do, I would support one hundred percent. But it was important that the decision was hers without any outside influence from the media, Nolan, or me.

SARIAH

WHEN HARPER'S NANNY DROPPED ZANDER OFF AT MY suite, I felt woefully prepared. Even though I'd been planning all week for his visit. I had snacks and I bought a gaming system with popular games. The hours I'd clocked on Google searching what eight-year-old boys liked to do was ridiculous. My exhaustive research led me to video games and Legos. So I purchased a massive Lego set that we couldn't possibly put together before he had to return home. We were having a sleepover, which now that I was staring at his big brown eyes, seemed a bit ambitious.

Zander's nanny handed me his backpack and wished me luck before leaving me all alone with a child. I wanted to call out and beg her to stay just until we were acclimated, but with fear in my eyes, I watched as she made her way down the hall and boarded the elevator.

Turning my attention to Zander, I asked, "How have you been?"

"Good."

"I'm really excited we're having this sleepover. I have some fun stuff planned."

"Cool." He scanned the space, sizing it up.

Leading us to the living room, I pointed to the stack of games. "Maybe you could pick one and then show me how to play?"

His face lit up, which helped to ease my breathing. I glanced at my phone screen. It had been five minutes and his mother wasn't picking him up until nine in the morning. Regret was the overarching theme of the night. Why did I agree to jump into the brother and sister bonding time with no buffer? Maybe we should've started out with something less overwhelming, like a playdate in the park.

"Do you like pizza?"

"Yes," he said, freeing a game from its plastic wrap.

"Great. I'm going to order pizza. What kind of toppings do you like?"

"Pepperoni, pineapples, and bell peppers."

I wrinkled my nose. "Okay, so I'll order one yucky pepperoni, pineapple, and peppers pizza and then a meat lover's pizza which actually tastes good."

Zander chuckled. "My mom doesn't like pineapples on pizza either."

"That's because it's gross."

"Just more for me then."

After ordering the pizzas, I listened while Zander tried to explain the objective of a game with a really fast hedgehog. The doorbell chimed and I hopped up to answer it. *The pizza spot must be having a slow night because our food was here in record time.* On the other side of the door, it wasn't my pizzas but something just as hot.

"Hey," Justus said with an effortless smile before planting a quick kiss on my lips.

"What are you doing here?"

"It's time for Coach Chappel Academy."

"Is that today?" I stood in front of the door as he shifted his head trying to get a look inside. In the midst of my sleepover preparations, our prescheduled Ramblers 101 session completely skipped my mind.

"Did you forget about me?"

"It's been a crazy week." I offered up an apologetic smile.

"Can I come in?"

"Umm …"

"Umm?" Justus's eyebrows inched up his forehead at the unexpected and less than enthusiastic response.

"My brother's here."

"Okay, can I come in or nah?"

"You can but I don't think we'll get much studying done."

He moved his hands like scales. "Studying or being able to stare at you in reverent admiration. Either will work."

I giggled, stepping aside to let him in.

When Zander caught sight of Justus, he jumped up and a broad smile spread across his face. "Coach Justus."

"Z-man how have you been?" Justus and Zander performed a complicated handshake involving spins and fist bumps.

"Z-man? Wait, you two know each other?"

"Yeah, Grover would bring Zander to the training facility all the time. Zander's an honorary Rambler." Justus's gaze landed on the TV. "What do we have over here? Is that Sonic?"

The news of my father allowing Zander to tag along with him to the office was surprising. I looked at my eight-year-old brother with curiosity, wondering what his experience with our dad was like. Harper said my father wanted to try to get the parenting thing right this go round. Maybe that meant my dad was more of a present father for Zander.

It's wild how two people could be raised by the same man and their impression of that man could be vastly different. I hoped Zander's time with my father was better than mine. I'd be lying if I didn't admit I was jealous. Sounds like Zander received the best of Grover Thornton while I had to survive on scraps.

When the pizza arrived, we devoured it and Zander dared me to try a pineapple topped slice and I was forced to concede it wasn't half bad. After pizza, Zander played with the remote-controlled car. Justus set up obstacles out of paper cups and Zander tried to maneuver around them. That little boy was the spitting image of my brother Benji. Zander's complexion was a few shades lighter, but other than that, he could be Benjamin's twin. The resemblance was one of the many reasons I'd avoided spending time with Zander. Seeing his face was a reminder of my late brother. I missed him so much and being around Zander just made my heart ache deeper.

I would give up everything, all the money, all the success to have my brother back. Shit, I'd give up my very soul if it meant he got to live the life he so rightly deserved. Benji was two years younger than me, but by the time he entered high school, it was difficult to make the distinction. He was the all-American kid, athletic, smart, and rich. Extremely well liked and popular. He was kind to everyone. Benji was supposed to graduate from college and make this world a better place.

"Okay per your mother you need to be in bed by ten and it's already past eleven. So wash up and I'll turn down your bed." I hated to be the party pooper, but I wanted to follow the list of rules Harper emailed over to me. No sweets after nine. No soft drinks. No PG-13 shows. It was like having a sleepover with Gizmo from those Gremlins movies.

Zander tried to negotiate, but as a seasoned business professional, I didn't compromise. In the second bedroom, I tucked Zander in and turned on a night light.

"Good night," I said, heading for the door.

"Wait, you have to read me a story," Zander objected.

"Why would I do that?"

"Because my dad read me a story every night."

"I find that hard to believe. Plus Dad traveled. He was never home."

"When he was away, he would call or video chat."

When I tell you my jaw dusted the floor. Who was this man who doted on his kid and made an effort to ensure Zander had sweet dreams each night? "I don't know any kid stories." My shoulders hopped.

"Tell me a story about you and my dad."

"Alright." I took tentative steps back to the bed, sitting on the edge. "My dad … our dad, he loved being by the water. My favorite memories were when we went to the lake house. Did he ever take you and your mom?"

Zander's head swept left to right, indicating a no. Which made sense. When I was reviewing the assets I inherited, I was surprised to find the lake house listed among them. I'd always assumed he'd sold it years ago.

"I think I enjoyed the lake house because it was secluded and there were very few distractions. Dad grew up in the city but he had an appreciation for nature. It's weird something as simple as viewing the stars at night can be a luxury. He loved the silence; he found it peaceful. At home it was always so busy. He was always on the go, but at the lake house it was like time didn't exist. It was always magical to me.

"One summer we built a treehouse. Every morning we'd gather our tools and get to building. Just Dad, Benji, and me. I think we got in his way more than anything. Benji was around your age and I was probably ten. Even when we made a mess or acted silly he never lost patience with us.

"When I was younger, I thought Daddy was a God. He was so strong he could lift me and Benji at the same time. He taught me how to hammer in a nail. And when I missed and hit my hand by accident my daddy held me close, rocking me back and forth until the tears dried up."

I turned to look at Zander and he was fast asleep. Which was probably for the best because my chest was tight and I had to swallow hard several times to work the emotion threatening to spill out back down my throat. Brushing Zander's forehead, I stood to leave the room and found Justus leaning against the doorjamb.

"Are you okay?" His normally serene face was marred with concern.

"I'm fine." I forced a smile.

Back in the living room, I convinced Justus to start our study session. It was late and I didn't want to be alone. But more importantly I needed a distraction. I followed along in my binder as he discussed various game plays, only catching every other word because I was unable to focus.

"Why are your eyes glazed over? Am I going too fast?"

I patted his arm. "No. I'm sorry."

Justus shut his binder. "Do you want to talk about whatever it is that's stressing you out?"

"It's nothing."

"You've been preoccupied the entire night."

I released a strangled breath. "It's just that Zander looks exactly like my brother Benji. Sometimes when he talks I have to do a double take. How can he be so similar, same mannerisms, same crooked smile when they never even met?"

"You and your brother were pretty close, huh?"

"He was my best friend."

Justus cupped his hand around my neck, rubbing

softly. "What happened to him, if you don't mind my asking?"

"The lake. That fucking lake house." The place that held so many fond memories also was the scene of the worst experience of my life. I thought about Benji often, although I hardly ever spoke about him. Right after he passed, I wanted to talk about him but it became clear the mention of his name was too painful for my family, so I shifted into silent mode, never really allowing myself to go through the grieving process.

"It was spring break. Benji was a sophomore in college and I was a senior. We went to the lake house with family and friends like we'd done so many times in the past. Benji and I were goofing around trying to see which one of us could swim the furthest. We didn't realize how far from shore we were until it was too late. We got caught in a rip current. The lake was so serene when we jumped in. I don't even know where it came from. It pulled us further and further from shore. I tried grabbing his hand but was too turned around to latch on. Benji looked drained from trying to fight against the current.

"He screamed out to me 'Swim Sariah ... swim toward shore.' I turned my attention to the shoreline and focused on swimming with all my might. I thought he was behind me ... just right behind me. But when I got to the shore he was nowhere to be seen. I cried out calling his name before stumbling to the house for help. My dad and the other men took the boat out looking for him. But he was gone. It would take three days and several divers before his body was recovered."

Justus grabbed at my hands restraining me. "Sariah, stop. Baby calm down."

I'd been clawing at my skin and had drawn blood. My shoulders were rounded into a heap, as if I were trying to disappear into myself. A familiar thread of guilt tugged at my rib cage. In an attempt to steady my voice, I swallowed hard, hoping to push down the tears threatening to overflow. I wasn't okay. Nothing was ever okay after Benji died. His death forever changed our family.

"Benji died because of me. I was his big sister. I was supposed to protect him. I failed. My father never forgave me for it. And I don't blame him," My tone was dull. This was a fact I'd accepted years ago.

Justus scooped me in his massive arms and pressed me against his chest, holding me tight.

"It's all my fault. It's my fault." I welcomed the hug, clinging to him. Being vulnerable was something I tended to avoid, but I half wished I could open the valve and release the decade or so of built-up pressure. Justus just held me tighter, allowing me to melt into him. I buried my face into his neck and let go.

Rita, my mother's longtime housekeeper, answered the door with a smile. "Sariah, what a pleasant surprise." She pulled me into an embrace. One that I wallowed in for far too long, still raw from the outpouring of emotion last night.

Rita escorted me to the living room where my

mother was knitting. Her face lit up when she saw us enter the room. "What are you doing here?"

"I was in the neighborhood."

"I'll go put on some coffee and prepare a plate of pastries," Rita said, leaving us alone.

"Since when do you knit?" I asked.

"Just because I'm old it doesn't mean I can't learn new tricks." My mother was sixty-seven but she didn't look her age. She was a former supermodel who graced the covers of Ebony, Jet, Essence, and Vogue. With an active social calendar and a handful of suitors, she was living the second half of her life to the fullest. My mom didn't hug me; she knew unnecessary displays of affection made my skin crawl. But right about now I was jonesing for one of her full-bodied hugs while she gently rubbed my back.

"Mom?"

"Hmm?" She looked up from her yarn and registered the distress in my face. Standing, she gave me exactly what I needed. As she enveloped me in her arms and I crumbled. "Baby, what's wrong?"

I was sobbing again, unable to form sentences.

"Sariah, you're scaring me. What's going on?"

Rita returned with a carafe of coffee and quietly set the tray on a nearby table before leaving us once again.

My mother led me to the couch and I practically sunk into it.

"Talk to me." She clasped her hands around mine.

"I miss him. We spent so much time being mad and now ..." I licked at my upper lip. "He probably died thinking I hated him."

"You get your stubborn demeanor from your father. He regretted how things ended up."

"Why didn't he say something?"

"Have you read his letter?"

I wiped my eyes. I'd forgotten all about the letter my mother gave me months ago. "Did you read it?"

"I was tempted but no. It was addressed to you."

"What if the letter just confirms everything I always suspected?"

My mother reached for a handful of Kleenex, passing them to me. "You think your daddy wrote you a letter saying you aint shit?"

I shrugged. It was unlikely but not impossible.

"Maybe his note can provide you the closure you need," my mother offered.

That was something I was in desperate need of. It was as if my life was filled with unfinished chapters. I was in a constant state of limbo waiting for a resolution. My father's death should've tied up all the ragged loose ends into a messy bow, but no such luck. Inhaling courage, I asked the question I wanted the answer to most. "Do you blame me for Benji's death?"

My mother smoothed the hairs framing my face. "Darling child, where is this all coming from?"

"It's just that everything changed after that. You and daddy started having problems. He was traveling more than ever. When you two eventually divorced he made no effort to actually see me. There was just so much hurt and pain and none of us knew how to work our way through it."

I spotted a glimmer of unshed tears in her eyes.

"When Benji died a piece of me died with him. I wanted to curl into a ball and just give up. But I had you. My precious girl. And I had to be strong for you. When we lose someone we love, the thought of moving on can be scary and it almost feels like a betrayal to them in some way. But move on we must." She grabbed my chin, making sure I was looking in her almond-shaped eyes. "Never, not for one second did I ever blame you for what happened. Do you understand me?"

I nodded my head as tears silently fell down my cheeks. Her words were like a blanket wrapping around me to keep me warm and protected. In the midst of my contentious relationship with my father, Momma Thornton was always there for me. She was present for every milestone. Never forgot to call on special occasions. She'd always had my back and I felt silly for doubting her deep-rooted love for me. My mother poured coffee and handed me a chocolate chip scone. After a few minutes, the nutty roast and sweet treat helped soothe my spirit.

My features lit up with the realization I had news to share. "Guess who slept over at my place last night?"

"Who?"

"Zander, we had a sleepover."

"All night?"

I giggled. "That's usually what a sleepover entails."

"How'd it go?" She laid a linen napkin on my lap, ever mindful of crumbs.

"It was terrifying at first but then less so after we got to know one another. It also helped that Justus was there to act as a buffer?"

"Justus?"

I realized this was the first time my mother had heard me utter that name. I considered my next words carefully. "Justus Chappel, the coach for the Ramblers."

"And what was he doing at your place?"

"He's a friend." A friend that made my coochie quiver.

"A friend?"

"Mom, please don't."

"I didn't even say anything. I'm just glad you have a *friend* looking out for you."

"Anyway. I think I'm going to schedule another playdate with Zander soon."

"Was this your idea?"

"No. Harper suggested it. She wants Zander to be connected to Dad's side of the family."

My mother flashed me a cautious eye. "And you don't think that has anything to do with getting closer to the Thornton fortune?"

"I thought that too at first but she seemed sincere so I'm going to leave it at that."

"When do I get to meet your boyfriend?"

"Nice try. He's not my boyfriend."

Yet.

JUSTUS

ONCE IN A WHILE, I WAS REQUIRED TO DON A MONKEY SUIT and attend a charity event or some random party where everyone stood around patting each other on the back. Tonight, I was getting all dressed up for an NBA hosted party being held at the Wynn Casino. Another perk to living in Vegas was the league loved to host events in our city. The rented space at the Wynn was converted into a gambling floor. It wasn't an original theme, but the space was still impressive.

When I walked in, I was handed a stack of chips which I slipped in the pocket of my plum hued suit. After all, I was in Vegas and a black suit was considered pedestrian. Scattered among the well-dressed crowd were gambling tables and slot machines. The room opened up to a lush outdoor space with a large covered gazebo decorated in twinkle lights. Lo-fi jazzy music floated in between the conversations that filled the room.

I spotted Klay at the bar and headed in his direction.

"Coach, looking good," Klay said with a dap.

"Thank you. You're looking dapper as well."

"What are you drinking?"

"I'm going to start out easy with some seltzer water."

Klay added my drink request with his and I waited, scanning the room to determine who to avoid and who I looked forward to talking to. My head panned to the entrance just at the moment of Sariah's arrival. As expected, she looked stunning, snatching the air from my chest. She was wearing a one shoulder dark green, form-fitting dress with a high slit. The way the material clung to her ample curves forced drool to pool at the corners of my mouth. Her thick hair was slicked into a sleek ponytail and around her neck was a chunky gold choker necklace.

As she made her way through the room, I was treated with a side view of her ample ass. The same ass my face was submerged in last night. An ass I hoped to grab hold of later on this evening. When she spotted me staring, my heart ceased. The corners of her mouth curled into a naughty grin and I was reminded of her many pleas to be finger fucked harder while she choked on my dick. Turning my attention back to Klay, I knew the balls of my cheeks were rosy and I needed a distraction to prevent my dick from tenting my pants.

A gentle hand touched my back and was followed by a familiar voice that always caused the goose pimples to raise on my arms. "Hello gentleman. May I say you two are looking very sharp." Sariah's voice was like a song.

Klay tipped his glass with a goofy smile. "As do you."

"Klay, didn't you promise me an introduction to your wife?"

"That I did. I'll go and wrangle her up. She is looking forward to meeting you." Klay scurried away on a mission to locate his wife in the gigantic space.

Sariah ordered a white wine before looking up at me. "You look nice, Coach."

"You look good enough to eat."

"Well that is my plan." She bit her lips. I shoved my hands in my pockets so I wouldn't accidentally touch her. "I was hoping you'd ask me to be your date for tonight's event. But the invitation never came."

"I just didn't want to make things complicated for you."

"So you were looking out for me?"

"Yes."

"What if I like complicated?" An innocent observer from across the room would be scratching their head trying to figure out what Sariah and I were up to. We were standing closer than acquaintances and appeared overly familiar with one another.

I leaned in with a chuckle. "No, you told me your life was already too complicated. So I'm not looking to add to that."

She and I were in this weird gray area. Where we weren't official but things weren't casual. The only reason I hadn't asked Sariah to be my girlfriend was because I wasn't sure a committed relationship was what she wanted. Not once had she mentioned an interest in anything more. She didn't even live in Vegas full time. But now she was expressing regret that we didn't attend this event together.

"Well maybe I'm ready for you to fuck all that up."

"I'm not interested in making things harder for you. I want to make your life better. With me I want there to be more happy days than sad ones. That's what I'm offering."

"Occasional happiness."

"When you put it like that it sounds horrible."

"If it's with you … it sounds divine."

The compulsion to kiss her was overwhelming. I couldn't recollect ever wanting anything more in my life. I was ready to pull up to the negotiation table and finalize this agreement. If you promise to hold my hand when I reach for yours, I promise to let you place your cold feet up against me. If you promise to kiss me good morning when you wake up, I promise to cuddle with you until you fall asleep each night.

"I'm just following your lead. If you want more, all you have to do is ask."

"I want—" Sariah's next words were interrupted by Nolan.

"Hello my dear. You look lovely as ever." He reached for her hand. "There are several people very eager to meet you." He pulled Sariah away, not even acknowledging me or apologizing for the theft of her attention. I silently seethed as Nolan led Sariah to a group of NBA executives, introducing her like he'd discovered her. Flagging down the bartender, I ordered a vodka gimlet and headed outside. I was reduced to walking around aimlessly, striking up conversations with other coaches in attendance and a few players.

For the next hour, I stumbled in and out of conversations about yachts and expensive trips. I walked up to one group of men discussing ways to hide funds from their spouses before filing for divorce. I'd never been happier to be legally unattached as I was at that moment. During my divorce from Melody, even though we tried to be civil, there was a rough patch where the process became acrimonious with us saying things to one another that to this day I still regret.

Getting remarried wasn't top on my to do list. But finding a woman to spend time with was important. The possibility that Sariah was willing to be that woman left me hopeful. We didn't need to rush the church and white dress just yet. All I was asking for was a chance to love her in a way I sensed she hadn't yet experienced. I got the impression that she was cautious when it came to her heart, holding parts of herself back for safekeeping.

I was pulled from my thoughts when I noticed both Nolan and Derek Wayne talking to Sariah. These fuckers where not going to use this event to further their nefarious plan. Not when I was nearby to squash it. Maneuvering through the crowd, I made my way to the inner circle and inserted myself into their conversation. "Hello gentleman, I hope you're not boring Sariah with talk of the glory days."

"Coach Justus, it's good seeing you again," Derek greeted me.

"You as well." We exchanged a handshake in which

his grip was unnecessarily firm in an attempt to assert his dominance.

"I was just telling your lovely boss it should be a crime for owners to look this beautiful."

I fashioned my teeth into a smile.

"So Sariah, now that you own a basketball team, how are you finding things? I would imagine it's quite different from being in the beauty business."

"Different yes. But my father always taught me the nature of business was often universal."

"Ahh Grover, I miss the crazy bastard," Nolan said.

"Speaking of, allow me to extend my deepest sympathies for your loss." Derek reached out rubbing Sariah's arm which made my blood boil.

"Thank you."

"So what are your plans for the organization? If you don't mind me asking."

"I do mind." Her response took Derek by surprise.

"I understand wanting to hold things close to the vest but seeing how you are in virgin territory it may be helpful to have a seasoned professional guide you." His eyes were salacious and he didn't even try to hide it as his gaze slid down the length of her long body.

"I'm sure you'd just love to guide me through it." Sariah's tone implied she was not impressed by the three-time MVP.

I wanted to speak up but didn't want it to appear like she wasn't capable of handling the conversation.

"Sometimes a woman just needs to be talked through it," Derek said.

"A woman?"

"Yes, basketball is a male dominated sport. I'm not trying to be misogynistic, it's just a fact."

"Are you implying that because I'm a woman it would be harder for me to run the organization?"

Derek held his hand up apologetically. "Look Sariah, I'm sure you are capable at many things but running a team is an entirely different beast."

No longer able to hold my tongue, I spoke up. "Some would say that being a player doesn't necessarily equip someone to own a team."

"You can't be serious." Nolan tsked.

"Bates, Roydell, Spencer. All great players who turned out to be horrible owners," I said.

"I've dedicated my entire life to this sport. I know what's required to win," Derek scoffed.

Sariah cleared her throat. "And you think a former player would be better suited to handle the Ramblers?"

"I'm saying we all have lanes and maybe it's best that you stay in yours."

The vein in my forehead pulsed. *Was this Nolan's idea of a subtle take over?* Derek was practically suggesting she sign her rights away on a cocktail napkin. "Sariah is the owner of the Ramblers; she doesn't really need to justify anything."

"I'm sure our owner is very capable but if the team doesn't continue to succeed, she'll have a lot of explaining to do," Nolan chimed in.

Sariah flashed Nolan a dubious look before asking, "Derek, do you own a team?"

"No I don't."

"Ahh ... I see. I do agree with you on one point. It's

smart to surround myself with other successful team owners. And seeing how I'm the only real owner currently in this conversation I will see myself out." Sariah excused herself, leaving me with the two knuckleheads.

When she was out of earshot, I asked. "What the hell was that?"

"It was a conversation." Nolan took a long swig from his glass.

Scanning the room, I lowered my voice not wanting to be overheard. "It felt more like an ambush. I thought the plan was to persuade Sariah to sell the team?"

"Now she knows there are others gunning for her position," Derek said with a nonchalant hop of his broad shoulders. "Like Grover, it appears she understands how to play hardball. But in the end she won't know what hit her."

"She's not smart enough to figure out she's in way over her head. The girl is drowning and we are prepared to throw her a life vest," Nolan agreed.

He wasn't offering a life vest, he was launching a harpoon. "It's never smart to underestimate your opponent. If anyone should understand that it should be you, Derek."

"Sariah isn't competition. She's the prey being led to the slaughter."

I wanted to punch this oversized, overrated, out of touch bastard in the face. Right now they believed I was on their side and it was best to keep letting them think that. If they shared their plan, I could work to shut them down. My lips torqued into a slight grin. "Listen I just want us to be careful with how we play this. Because if Sariah starts to suspect a double cross is in the works, she will cut that shit off at the knees."

"Don't worry, she's too distracted with her makeup business and her life in New York to care about what we have planned." Nolan rapped me on the shoulder. "Great job playing Team Sariah. That was good thinking. Right now Derek is the bad guy and you and I fully support the young Ms. Thornton. I knew it was smart to hook you in."

I did my best to conceal my disgust. After all Grover Thornton had done for Nolan, his loyalty ran thin. He should be Sariah's biggest cheerleader. Turns out he was her number one hater.

AFTER A FEW MORE HOURS OF DINNER AND MINGLING, I was ready to call it a night. I sent Sariah a text asking her to meet me at the valet. When she arrived, I pretended to be surprised by her appearance. "Do you need a ride home Ms. Thornton?"

"I was going to call my driver. But if you're headed that way a ride would be great."

The drive home consisted of Sariah singing off key to every song, her body taunting me as she swayed back and forth. When we pulled into the garage, she bolted from the car. "I have to pee."

Disarming the alarm, I followed her discarded shoes and purse to my bedroom.

"So that Wayne guy is a world class douche," Sariah called from the bathroom.

"I don't disagree."

"Did you see the way he looked at me?" she asked, reentering the bedroom.

"I did."

"Gross. He used to be a player?"

"Yeah, a really good one. Jordan, Wayne, Kobe."

"So what's he up to now?"

"He has a few business ventures that have been really lucrative." I sat on the ottoman in front of the bed and unlaced my dress shoes.

"I don't even get why he was there." She removed her jewelry. I loved the unceremonious way she placed her items on the dresser. It was as if being here with me in my space was second nature to her.

"Because he's basketball royalty and that carries weight in the industry."

"I guess."

"It sounds like he's interested in being a part of an organization." I critically scanned her face to gauge her reaction to my words.

"Hmm. Well good luck to him with that attitude."

"Basketball is all about honoring the legends. I'm sure there are several teams that would love to have him as part of the staff."

"Are you suggesting the Ramblers should be one of those teams?" Sariah turned, gesturing for me to unzip her dress.

"No, I'm not."

I wanted to tell her about Nolan conspiring with Derek, but I didn't want to upset her over something that honestly could never happen. Sariah held majority ownership; it would take an act of God to change that. She was already overwhelmed by the loss of her father and the inheritance, although she was putting on a brave face. Why burden her with this too? But I didn't want to leave her with a blind spot, she needed to know what Nolan was scheming to do.

"Baby, I've been meaning to talk to you about No …" Sariah dropped her evening gown to reveal her lacey embroidered undergarments. The thong had a bow at the top of her ass. Which was appropriate because that ass was a gift from God.

"Do you want to go for a swim?" she asked innocently.

I didn't utter a word, just shed articles of clothing one by one until I was buck naked. Scooping her in my arms, I opened the bedroom sliding door and cannon-balled us into the pool. When we popped to the surface, she had a mischievous glint in her eye.

"I didn't like seeing all the women at the party flirting with you all night."

I laughed. "No one was checking for me. My pockets aren't deep enough." I'd amassed wealth but, in a room filled with billionaires like Sariah, I was the low man on the pole.

"You think not, huh? In the ladies' room a redheaded woman gushed about you. And how happy she was that you were in Vegas as part of the Ramblers' organization. She claimed hands down you were the hottest coach in the league—"

"Okay I don't need to hear any more." I knew exactly who Sariah was referring to.

"But I haven't gotten to the best part. She said your dick was magical. And that after fucking you she felt like a new woman."

"Hmm …" I shook my head.

"So you like redheads?" Sariah quipped.

"Stop it. That was years ago. One-night stand." I smoothed the wet tendrils of hair from her face and forehead. "I like you, that's what I like."

"Not going to lie, I was jealous. Of course you've been with other women. I just didn't expect to be meeting them at company events."

"I'm sorry."

"I don't get jealous. So I had to ask myself why this totally innocuous fact about you upset me. Which led me to the conclusion that I care for you … deeply. Once I moved past the initial shock of falling for a man, I determined what I needed to do to keep your magical Johnson all to myself."

"What did you end up coming up with?" I unhooked her bra, letting it float away.

"I don't like sharing. I don't even like the possibility I might have to share. So tell me Justus, am I sharing you?"

"Everything I have belongs to you. My heart and my dick."

Sariah's eyes pinged across my face, searching for falsehoods. Her breathing was shallow. "I was thinking … maybe I could look for a place more permanent in Veg—"

My lips crashed into hers, silencing her sentence. Words escaped me and none were suitable enough to convey how happy the thought of her being in Vegas on a regular basis made me. I would just have to show her exactly how I felt. She slipped her thong over her bodacious backside while I reached for a water inflatable shaped like a popsicle with a bite removed, and positioned Sariah's torso on top. Swimming up to her from behind, I slid inside, her whimpers of pleasure letting me know she could feel every inch. I rocked my hips while pulling the floaty back and forth. Sariah reached back, sinking her nails into my forearm.

Her hips wiggled while mine rolled and as the momentum built, her vocal appreciation did as well. "Oh shit baby take it. You always know just what I need."

My hands coasted up her back and I wrapped the length of her ponytail in my hand, using it as a rein to guide her movements. As her backside slammed into me, she cried out begging me not to stop, but I had to. What was the point of fucking this goddess if I couldn't witness her big mink eyes ignite with desire every time I hit her spot? We floated over to the steps of the pool and I sat on the second step so we were only partially submerged. With her on top, I had the vantage point I most desired. I buried my face into her chest, feasting on her breast while she fucked me. Her ass worked overtime as she twerked on top of me.

"You smell so good," I said, before moving on to her other nipple. "You feel even better." My hands massaged her back before sliding to her ass to help her maneuver my length.

Sariah lowered her face in my neck, sucking until she branded me. "Your dick truly is magical. I can't get enough," she half joked.

I changed my stroke pattern and her pupils met the back of her head and her whole-body vibrated. "Whose dick is it?"

She grabbed my chin and without hesitation professed. "Mine."

"Prove that shit."

Sariah was not a woman who liked to be challenged. She braced her hands on my knees and fucked me so good I swear I died and her wet pussy brought me back to life, sending a shock wave to my dick. This woman had my teeth chattering in a heated pool. My heartbeat was throbbing in my ears and acted as the bass line for Sariah's screams of pleasure. Her body convulsed and I had to cradle her head to stop it from being submerged under water. I lifted her toward me, kissing her bee sting lips. Her eyes twitched as she was in the thick of her orgasm.

"I love it when you come for me," I whispered.

Sariah's eyes slammed into mine and her body crumbled as she cried out trembling against me. That look in her eyes was all the motivation I needed. I grabbed hold of her waist and released all my love inside of her.

When our bodies finally stopped twitching, Sariah grabbed hold of my beard. "Say it, so I can say it back." Her gaze was almost pleading.

I caressed her cheek, needing no additional prompting. "I love you Sariah Thornton and I'm convinced I always will."

Her lips pinched upward. "I know logically we can't possess or own other people. But I am completely yours. I love you," she whispered over my lips. Her breath hitched like the last three words caught her by surprise.

Life is funny. You can be existing, perfectly content and happy and then randomly meet a person who changes how you see the world and shifts the things you find most important. Sariah was that for me. This person was everything I didn't know I needed and craved. And now the thought of living life without her was unfathomable.

SARIAH

I'VE BEEN IN LOVE THREE TIMES. FIRST IN HIGH SCHOOL with Ralph Morrison. I just knew we were destined to be together forever until we went off to college and long distance and a plethora of options made staying together difficult. My next great love began in my twenties and ended well into my thirties. When we called it quits, I was heartbroken and vowed not to give myself over to anyone ever again.

Now here I was years later, casually handing my heart and soul to yet another man. But to be fair, Justus wasn't just any man. He was the first man who made my insides shimmer. I was happy all the time. My thoughts of him made me smile, and the anticipation of seeing him again made my heart race. In the last several weeks since we made it semiofficial, I'd found myself humming an unfamiliar tune like some chick in a rom-com movie.

It was a random Friday morning and Justus was knocked out next to me. Normally he'd be up by now but his flight got in late last night from Philadelphia. Climbing out of bed, I decided to let him rest a bit longer. In the kitchen, I found the twins finishing up their breakfast.

"Morning," I said.

"Good morning," the twins replied in unison.

I shuffled from the fridge, to the cabinet, to the coffee maker.

"Ask her," I heard Ebony whisper.

"Ask me what?" I examined one pretty brown face then the other. After spending considerable time with Justus and the girls, I could now easily tell the two apart. Their facial expressions were quite distinct. Jhené was far more animated when she talked. Now if the two were standing silently side by side, I might still have a bit of trouble.

Jhené cleared her throat. "We were wondering if you wanted to go shopping with us this weekend to pick out accessories for the dance?"

Their school was hosting a formal dance and both girls were attending with a group of friends. Last Sunday they were so excited to show me the dresses they'd purchased while shopping with their mom. I was just as eager as them asking for a fashion show. We talked at length about shoes and other accessories, but I never thought I would get the invite to tag along while they shopped for them.

"What about your mom?" The last thing I wanted to do was step on any toes.

"She's going to some art thing out of town. Dad was supposed to take us but we'd much prefer to go with someone who has actual style," Ebony said.

"I have style. Thank you very much." Justus limped

into the room looking as if he could use a few more winks.

The twins rolled their eyes.

"Who doesn't enjoy shopping. I'd love to go. Thanks for the invite."

"Girls, I called a car to take you to school so finish getting ready," Justus said, wrapping his arms around me.

They dumped their cereal bowls in the sink and headed to their rooms.

"Good morning," he said.

"Good morning. You look like shit."

"I feel like it."

Justus had been battling a cold for over a week. As I played caregiver, I learned he was a horrible patient and didn't listen to my pleas for him to stay in bed and rest. He smoothed back the hair piled atop my head in a messy bun. Leaning in, he kissed my forehead and I enveloped him in an embrace, pulling him closer. I missed him when he traveled for work. He'd been on the road for three days. Three days of sleeping alone. Three days of not kissing his beautiful face.

Justus's phone rang, alerting him the car was out front. "Come on, let's go," he yelled.

The twins came rushing down the hall. Each girl gave me a hug goodbye before heading out the door with their father. After seeing them to the car, Justus walked back to the kitchen and I handed him a cup of coffee.

He took a long sip before speaking again. "I'm off all day."

"Hmm …"

"I was thinking maybe we could spend the day in bed. Watch old movies, eat, take some cat naps." His fingers played with the pendant attached to my necklace.

"I can't I have a meeting with Nolan and the merchandising team." I pouted.

"You're the boss, cancel it. Spend the day with me. I promise I'll make it worth your while"

I didn't need much convincing. A boring meeting with Nolan or being laid up with Justus for the day. Grabbing my phone from the counter, I sent my secretary a text telling her I was feeling under the weather and needed to reschedule. I didn't wait for a reply before turning my phone on do not disturb.

Back in the bedroom, Justus made me happy I chose to ditch work. He was devouring me with his tongue. Licking and slurping up my juices. One thing about me … this pussy stayed ready. Just the thought of him during a boring spot in my day saturated the seat of my drawers.

I pushed his head up and begged for him to fuck me right now. Justus laid back and I climbed on top. This was my favorite position because I was in control and was still able to greedily plant kisses on his lips. Rocking my hips, I gasped each time I hit the bottom of his shaft. Justus's hands were all over me, pinching my nipples, coasting along my back, and claiming hold of my waist. He applied pressure to my neck, pulling me toward his waiting lips. I sucked on his lower lip before plunging my tongue into his warm mouth. He moaned as our lips made love to each other. Pulling away, we both smiled.

Justus placed his thumb in my mouth and I worked my tongue around just how he liked. Removing his thumb, he slowly inched it into my ass, filling me. My core throbbed, the stimulation spurred on a hard orgasm that tore through me like a wrecking ball. I collapsed on top of him as he continued to thrust. The undulating pleasure radiating from my core was almost too much to bear. Each stroke caused a mini ripple effect that forced me to shiver and moan.

He found my lips kissing them hard before crying out for me. "Damnit Sariah." Which in my opinion was one of the sexiest things a man could do. Let me know how good it feels when you're inside me. After he fully released, his next kiss was softer and less urgent. I dismounted, resting my head on his chest.

"And that was just round one," I teased.

"Well if we're going multiple rounds. I'll need to eat something." He swung his legs off the side of the bed with a labored grunt that seemed to claim his breath.

I sat up with concern. "Is it your knee?

"Yeah, they're just sore from traveling. You know how they get." He rubbed at his left leg.

I'd witnessed his morning routine consisting of grunts and groans as he made his way out of bed. His movements sluggish because his muscles were sore and tight. Hot showers helped, but he was essentially living with muscle spasms and throbbing pain on a daily basis. And his weekly physical therapy sessions oftentimes left him spent and grouchy. Being folded up on a plane for hours also didn't help.

"Have you considered consulting a doctor about the pain?" I asked.

"I've met with several doctors."

"What do they suggest? Is there a different form of therapy they could try? Tracie hurt her back once and heat therapy worked."

"Therapy can only do so much. Some things can't be fixed."

"But baby, you're in pain. You shouldn't have to live like that."

Justus flashed an agitated glare in my direction. "Why does everyone think they know what's best for me? Deck, Pratt, my ex, and now you. Last time I checked you weren't a doctor, unless you inherited a PHD I don't know about."

My eyes narrowed as my lips pressed into a line. "I'm going to give you a pass because I realize you're in pain but I suggest you check your tone. I was only trying to help."

Justus released a weighty exhale. "You're right. I'm sorry. My knee is just a sore subject for me. No pun intended."

"Apology accepted." I rubbed his arm. The last thing I wanted was to pry, but I didn't enjoy watching the man I love suffer. "Are there any medications that could help you manage the pain?" His features tightened, despite his apology I got the sense he was still irritated. "You're clearly choosing not to say something. So just spit it out. I won't be offended."

"I'm going to need that in writing," he joked.

"You have my word."

"I've been dealing with this injury for years. It ended my basketball career. Do you really think I haven't considered all my options?"

"I'm not suggesting you haven't." I rose from the bed and threw on my robe. "I love you Justus and if you think I'm not going to speak on something that impacts your life you're mistaken. I want you to be happy and healthy and I want you to pursue all of your medical options no matter what the cost. If there's an experimental treatment not covered by your insurance that your doctor thinks could be successful then I've got you. I'll cover the expense. Money isn't an issue. All that matters is you."

Justus stood with a grunt shaking out his long limbs. Rounding the bed, he stopped in front of me. "I love you and I appreciate you wanting to take care of me. It's not a money issue, Sariah."

"So what is it?" I looked up at him, searching for answers. So much in my life was uncertain but maybe I could help solve this one thing.

"The potential solution involves surgery and that shit scares me."

"We can get the best surgeons in the world."

"Even the best make mistakes."

I cupped the back of his head pulling him close until our foreheads met. "I get it. I totally get it. Whatever you choose I'll support you. But can I ask a favor?"

"If it's in my power to provide it, I will."

"Can I come with you the next time you meet with

your doctor? I just want to hear their thoughts and maybe pick their brain. I may not have a PHD but I am habitually online and I've watched a bunch of videos about various knee injuries since meeting you and I have questions."

"You sound like my mother."

"Well then you know my concern is coming from a genuine place of love."

"Okay, I actually have an appointment scheduled for next week. I had some follow-up questions of my own regarding the surgery."

"I'll be there."

"Thank you," he whispered over my lips before planting a soft kiss.

"After we eat, I can give you a rub down."

"Who needs PT when I've got you?" He slapped my ass before heading toward the bathroom.

We pulled together breakfast with the remnants in the fridge. He was in desperate need of a grocery run. At the dining table, we sat in silence, both scrolling through our phones catching up on emails and missed messages. I balked at all the items that appeared to require my prompt response. My lawyers were working with my father's law firm to review all the business assets I'd inherited. Every day a new business summary report was in my inbox outlining the status of a company with its revenue, losses, and overall value.

I'd inherited huge holdings like the Ramblers, and then there were the smaller businesses like a string of gas stations scattered across the country. It would probably take me several years to fully evaluate all I now owned and the long-term viability of retaining the properties in my possession. Enfeebled by all the choices I was faced with; I tossed my phone on the table. Justus was thoughtfully chewing on a piece of toast while his eyes scanned the information on his phone.

"I went to a therapist the other day for the first time," I blurted out before shoving a forkful of eggs into my mouth."

"I didn't know you were in physical therapy."

"Not physical therapy. Therapy, therapy … with the couch and a trained medical professional jotting down notes." I canvassed his features for any hint of worry. Counseling often came with stigma. People assumed talking to a professional wasn't a sign of strength, but one of weakness. Do you know how many times I've been told to get over it? When someone hurt me deeply, when I lost my brother, or when my relationship with my father continued to come undone. Get over it. You're rich and pretty and so many people have it so much worse.

Justus placed his phone on the table, offering me his full attention. "Hmm, what made you want to do that?"

"Honestly, I think there's something wrong with me. And I don't really know how to work through it." I peeked at him over my coffee cup.

"Therapy's cool. I went when I had to retire early from playing ball. And then I went again after my divorce."

"So you don't think I'm weird?"

"No. Talking to someone impartial can be beneficial. I would also hope you'd feel comfortable enough to come to me. I can be a good listener. I won a best listening ears award in second grade. There was a ceremony and everything. I was very proud."

Amusement at the thought of a young Justus blushed my cheeks. "I do trust you. And that award was well deserved because you are a great listener. I just think the stuff with my dad and Benji ... I never really dealt with it, any of it. And these past couple of months it feels like all the hurt, anger, and sadness I buried deep down inside is now floating to the surface and I can't ignore it."

"And you're hopeful a therapist can help you navigate through some of that shit. It makes sense."

I examined his face for a long while before asking this next question. "Am I broken? Do you think I'm broken?"

"In what way?"

"My father has been dead for months and I've barely cried about it. I visited my mom and cried but I think those tears were more about me and less about losing him. Do you know what I mean?"

"Grief presents itself in different ways. There is no one size fits all."

"Hmm ..."

"Let me ask you this. Did you love your father?"

"Yes. I spent years searching for his approval. I wanted him to be proud of me. And now that he's gone it just feels like everyone is looking at me with disappointment in their eyes because I can't magically fill my father's shoes. My mother wants me to donate a large sum of money to her church. Harper wants me to step up and be a proper sister to Zander. My Aunt Dina asked me to give her the funds to open up her dream boutique." I was getting exhausted just thinking about all the new demands that were being placed on me.

"Just say no."

"It's not that simple."

"It's not that hard. Let's practice." He cleared his throat. "Sariah, can you loan me a billion dollars?"

"No." I smirked.

"See." He pointed at me. "If you can turn me down, and word on the curb is that I have a magical dick, if you can say no to me … you can say no to them."

I lifted my foot to his lap and rubbed it over his crotch. "Magically delicious," I agreed.

Justus claimed my foot and massaged it in his strong hands. If this coaching thing didn't work out he could have a successful career as a masseuse. His hands knew how to communicate multitudes of emotions without him having to utter a single word.

"My dad left me a letter."

"What did it say?"

"I don't know. I've had it for months and I'm too chicken shit to open it."

"What's the worst thing he could say?" His massage now included my ankle and calf.

"That he wished I was caught in the undertow instead of Benji." That would be the worst because that's the same thing I wished for each day.

"I think it's good that you're in therapy."

I released an incredulous laugh, playfully kicking his stomach with my foot.

"I didn't mean it like that. Stop laughing. I meant your father would have to be a fool if he didn't recognize how amazing you are. You built a company from the ground up and created one of the most successful beauty brands in the industry. You've also crafted a life for yourself that most can only dream about. You're smart and funny, and a great friend. You've made my life infinitely better since I met you. I can't imagine that letter saying any less than that. But if it does then fuck Grover Thornton."

I squared my shoulders. "You're right. I need to rip off the Band-Aid, read the stupid letter, and move on. Nothing he says or could say is going to change things at this point."

"I agree." Justus continued to massage my foot. My eyes fluttered closed and my head tilted to the side. I felt safeguarded when I was with him. He would never allow me to entertain negative self-talk or languish in doubt. Other than Benji, I'd never had a man support me like this. Justus grabbed my chair, pulling me closer to him. "You know I was thinking. If you wanted. You could move in here."

My eyes bulged from their sockets. "In your house?"

"Yeah, if you don't mind living with an old man and two loud teenagers." I think the shocked expression on my face prompted his next words. "Or not. No pressure."

"I just don't want to mess this up." I tugged at his T-shirt.

"Life is bound to get a little messy." He winked.

"What would Ebony and Jhené think?"

"They'd think it was about time. They want me to be happy. If you prefer, we could look for a new place."

"I love your place. It's cozy."

He wrinkled his nose.

"I like cozy. Your place feels like a home and I've never experienced that." I caressed the side of his face. "You don't think it's too soon?"

"No. But obviously you do. Which is fine. We can put a pin in it and circle back later."

"Are you sure?"

"Yeah, it's fine." He kissed my forehead before standing with a grunt. "I'm going to hop in the shower."

There was a big part of me that felt unworthy. Unworthy of this level of happiness. Living with Justus and having access to that man and his dick twenty-four seven would be a dream come true. But I didn't want to put that type of pressure on our relationship this early in the game. Dreams could only last for so long. And there were the twins to think about. Was I ready to be a stepmother? I was just starting to work through my family issues. Moving in was an aspirational goal. I just wanted to be the best version of myself for Justus and the girls.

JUSTUS

"I would've pushed to have us get together sooner if I knew I was going to get juicy stories about Justus," Sariah said with a laugh.

Deck's face lit up. "Can I tell her the one about the sisters in Kansas City?"

My eyes grew wide. "No."

"Wait a second, I want to hear the story," Sloane said, flashing her man a curious look.

"I'll tell you on the way home." He winked at her.

This was the first time Sariah and I were stepping out as a couple with some of my friends. It was important to me that we intermingled our lives. That meant spending time together with our respective friend groups. And eventually meeting one another's families. I was in this thing for the long haul, and I wanted to submerse myself in all things Sariah.

A double date with Deck and Sloane was an easy choice because both were laid back and they wouldn't pepper Sariah with a million questions. Well Deck wouldn't, Sloane on the other hand often said the first thing that came to her mind, oftentimes causing me to cringe. Sloane was nothing like the other basketball players' significant others. She was loud, with a no holds barred attitude, and she could drink me under the table. More importantly, she was fiercely protective of Deck. The two often got lost in their own world, laughing at jokes only they shared. It was endearing to see a big macho dude like Deck turn to mush for her.

"Is it weird dating your boss?" Sloane asked.

"I think we've managed not to let it get in the way too much," I said.

"I don't consider myself his boss." Sariah leaned into me with a nudge.

"But you are," Sloane said.

"I am, but we're a team."

"Don't get it twisted she is definitely the boss. She steals the covers and has to be in control of music selection in the car."

She pointed an accusatory finger. "That's because you say you don't care."

"I do care. But if it makes you happy to listen to the same Anjeni song on repeat fifty-eleven times, I'm going to roll with it because it puts a smile on your face." I imitated her singing one of Anjeni's song.

"I do not sound like that. I'm a good singer."

I flashed Deck a glance silently confirming she was no Whitney Houston.

"What about you, is it difficult being with a superstar basketball player?" Sariah asked.

Deck laughed. "Not so sure about the superstar part."

A crease cut across Sariah's forehead. "You're a great

player, Deion. I'm not well versed in sports, but I know talent when I see it. You pour out your heart on that court every night."

"Yeah, well tell that to Nolan," Deck scoffed.

"Okay I will." Sariah nodded her head with finality.

"What Nolan thinks doesn't fucking matter. Sariah's the owner and Nolan will have to fall in line." I was so tired of hearing that man's name. He was only the general manager because of Grover. I'm not saying he wasn't knowledgeable and business savvy, but he was also out of touch about what today's players were looking for. His only interest was making money. He didn't give a damn about the people that supported the organization.

In my opinion the Ramblers were only as strong as our weakest player. Our focus should be on investing in ways to help them thrive and grow. Nolan didn't even want to give a newbie a chance to get acclimated. He expected immediate results, but often a new player didn't show their potential until mid-season. Don't get me wrong, I'm here to win games, but to do that the players had to be cultivated, trained, and empowered.

"Nolan isn't bending the knee for no one. He was only loyal to your old man because Grover put him on," Deck said.

"He's been really nice and helpful to me," Sariah said without a hint of sarcasm.

Deck and Sloane gave me looks of disbelief at her trusting nature.

"We have better things to talk about than Nolan.

Let's get the night started with some drinks?" I suggested, flagging down the waiter.

When it was Sloane's turn to order she declined. "Nothing for me. I'm good with water."

My mouth turned into a sour line. "I've never known you to turn down an opportunity to turn up." Normally Sloane was the one goading me to try something other than my go to favorites. It dawned on me she'd passed on libations the last time we'd hung out.

"There's a first time for everything."

Narrowing my eyes, I sized her up. "Wait a minute. Are you …?"

Both Deck and Sloane displayed guilty smiles.

"Are you going to have a baby?"

Sloane nodded sheepishly.

I couldn't contain my excitement. Scrambling to my feet, I gave her a hug.

"Oh my God. Congratulations. How far along are you?" Sariah asked, the smile on her face almost as big as mine.

"We just passed our first trimester," Sloane beamed.

"It was a surprise. But it's the best surprise ever." Deck gave her lips a peck.

I spent the rest of the night trying to convince Deck and Sloane to name their bundle of joy after me, assuring them it was a unisex name. I couldn't be happier for my friend. Just a year ago I worried Deck was self-imploding and then he met Sloane, and everything changed. Life was full of surprises, and Deck having another child was one of the biggest.

On the ride home, I appreciated the perfect weather.

With the windows rolled down, the warm air was pleasant on my skin. Smooth jazz played in the background as the city zoomed past. Despite the great weather, full belly, and my beautiful date in the passenger seat, I couldn't shake Sariah's impression of Nolan. Clearing my throat, I gently squeezed her knee to gain her attention. "Sariah, about Nolan—"

She hissed out a breath of air. "No, it's date night. I don't want to talk about Nolan or the Ramblers."

"I just want you to have the full picture of the kind of man Busch is."

"It's clear you don't have positive things to say about Nolan. But your relationship with Nolan isn't mine. I've always believed in forming one's own opinion about a person and Nolan Busch is no different. I'm not naive; he's not being kind to me out of the goodness of his heart or because of his unwavering loyalty to my father. Maybe there is a conversation to be had about why I should keep my guard up, which for the record I have. But that conversation isn't going to happen tonight."

My jaw took on a stubborn bend. I was trying to look out for her, but she stated in no uncertain terms that I needed to mind my business. Maybe this was just one lesson she would need to learn on her own.

"You know what I do want to talk about?" She placed her hand on my penis, and it quickly came to life. The word of the night was horny. Which was nothing new because I was always lustfully fantasizing about new and exciting ways to get her to moan my name. "What does a woman have to do to get your dick in her mouth?" Sariah unzipped my pants and I practically liquified when she wrapped her hand around my naked dick. "Like I want to gag on it." She loved taunting me sexually, especially when I was in no position to act on it.

Grabbing her wrist, I placed her hand back in her own lap. "You do realize we're going to be home in five minutes, so you better suck up all this available oxygen. Because in a few minutes my dick is going to be blocking your airway."

"I'm counting on it."

As Sariah and I were waiting in Dr. Samuelson's office for my second consultation, my leg performed an anxious bounce. My scheduled appointment was timely because the other morning I was awakened by sharp shooting pains which locked my left leg as if in a twisting vise. This wasn't the first time this happened but it was the first time Sariah was present to witness it.

The cramping was so intense I fell from the bed and struggled to breathe. Sariah talked me through it until my muscles finally untethered. But the fear etched on her face was hard to get past. I'd been downplaying the discomfort in my knee, which was growing increasingly worse. I was lying to everyone. My physical therapist, my primary physician, but more importantly I'd been lying to myself. Acting as if ignoring it would make it somehow go away.

"Coach Chappel, it's great to see you again." Dr.

Samuelson approached with an outstretched hand.

"Hello." I pointed to Sariah. "This is my girlfriend Sariah."

"Hello, nice to meet you."

We exchanged pleasantries with the doctor peppering me with questions about the season and our playoff prospects. One thing about being a professional coach, people in this city were invested in the team and they wanted us to succeed. Sports teams and their cities had a funny relationship. Las Vegas residents were our biggest fans and our fiercest critics, but in the end we all wanted the same thing, a championship.

"I've got to say I'm surprised to see you again. The last time we spoke you seemed against having surgery."

"Yeah, well pain has a way of humbling us all."

"Are you going to tell her about what happened the other day?" Sariah whispered.

"I woke up in the middle of the night with searing pain in my leg. I couldn't bend my knee and it took several minutes for the spasms to release. That wasn't the first time this has happened, it's kind of normal."

"Normal? You were in tears. That's not normal," Sariah said.

"As you know Justus, the cartilage in your left knee is worn, we talking about bone on bone. Which is contributing to the pain and soreness you've described."

Sariah's face was lined with concern. "What are his options?"

That was the exact same question I'd asked years ago when I was first injured. What are my options? Back then I just wanted to heal and get back on the court.

"Surgery. We've reached the point where surgery is the best long-term solution."

This meeting was more to appease Sariah. I'd heard this all before. Surgery or bust. I'd run out of viable alternatives. We were now at the point of when … not if I had surgery.

"Of course we can continue to manage his pain with medication and physical therapy but over time it will be less effective. Long term, his posture and ability to walk long distances could be impacted."

Sariah's hand tightened around mine. "What's the risk with surgery?"

"Well with any surgery there are risks but knee replacement is a fairly common procedure and as I've told Justus he is in excellent physical condition, so recovery time shouldn't be a problem."

I zoned out while Sariah asked additional questions. It would be difficult to avoid surgery after Sariah's conversation with Dr. Samuelson. She would not let this go.

In the car, Sariah scanned the patient reference list Dr. Samuelson's assistant handed us on the way out. "What are you thinking?" she asked.

"I'm thinking I'm starving and we should get something to eat."

"I meant about what Dr. Samuelson said."

I rolled my shoulders. "Nothing I haven't already heard." Pulling into the parking lot of the first restaurant I saw, I placed the car in park.

"Justus—"

"The last time I had knee surgery I thought it would

fix me. But it just made things worse and two years after the surgery I couldn't play ball any longer."

"Dr. Samuelson said the procedure was routine. And if you don't feel comfortable with her, we can look into other surgeons."

I waved her words off. "Samuelson is a world-renowned specialist."

"So you're in good hands."

"I know seeing me groaning in pain on the floor was upsetting but I'm fine."

"Justus you were crying and gasping for air."

"I know you think this is an easy decision but I need to be one hundred percent sure. I have to get my house in order, update my will."

"Update your will? It's knee surgery."

"People die in surgery every day."

Sariah turned to face me, her irritation melting away. "Justus I'm in no way trying to downplay the very real fears you have about surgery. I understand your last operation did not turn out as planned. I know you think you can just push through the stiffness. But the reality is the pain is only going to worsen and quite honestly being in constant agony does something to a person. I know you're used to being the strong basketball player, but I just need you to feel better for the girls, for me, for your team. Whatever that looks like."

"What if something goes wrong?"

"What if it all goes right? Don't take my word for it. Talk to her former patients. Can you agree to that? Maybe hearing their experiences will help you make your mind up."

"I can do that."

Sariah rubbed lotion onto her hands while climbing into bed. She massaged the excess onto her neck and chest. This was our last night together. I was getting ready for a two-week stretch on the road. We had seven away games scheduled in the next two weeks.

"I've been reviewing some of my dad's business portfolios trying to decide what to sell and what to keep."

"Oh yeah?

"Did you know the Las Vegas location makes the Ramblers a more desirable team than others ranked higher than us?"

I did know that. Vegas was a social and entertainment hub. World class food, great shows, and amazing entertainment.

"Nolan thinks I could get close to three billion for it."

"If you were interested in selling."

Sariah remained silent.

"Are you seriously thinking about selling?"

"Well Nolan says—"

I sat up. "Fuck what Nolan says. What do you think?"

"I like the idea of owning a basketball team. But it demands being a priority and I can't devote that type of time right now."

"That's why you have a general manager."

"I don't trust Nolan to run the organization while

I'm focusing on Genuine Beauty."

"So you don't trust him to run the Ramblers but you trust his input regarding resale value."

Her reliance on Nolan was partially my fault because I allowed her to operate under the false assumption that Nolan was actually on her side. Was Nolan's plan working? Had he convinced Sariah selling the team was a win for all involved? There was no legal way for him to snatch control from her, so getting her to believe selling was her idea was the preferred method.

"No, I did my own research. I read that the New York Knicks have the highest valuation and like Vegas, that's more about the location, less about the actual team."

I knew I said I would stay out of this whole thing but she initiated this conversation. I was just asking important follow-up questions.

"Nolan doesn't have to be the general manager. You do know you can terminate his employment at any time."

"I know but it's just easier to have someone who's already familiar with the organization in place. One less thing to worry about."

I pinned my arms across my chest.

"What?"

"Nothing."

"You don't approve?"

"You don't need my approval."

"No you're right I don't."

At the end of the day the Ramblers were Sariah's to do with as she saw fit. Yes, she's my girlfriend, but she doesn't answer to me. And I've never asked that of her. I'm here to support her in any way she needs. I've been torn about speaking up and, in this moment, it dawned on me what I needed to do was stay in my fucking lane.

If Sariah came to me for advice of course I would provide it. But it wasn't my place to insert myself in the goings on at the Ramblers' organization beyond my role as the coach. If there was a problem at one of her other companies, I wouldn't toss in my two cents. Sariah was a capable business woman and a good judge of character. Eventually she'd see Nolan for exactly who he is.

Sariah grabbed her phone from the bedside table and scrolled in silence for several minutes. Even more confirmation I needed to mind the business that paid me. Any time we talked about Nolan and his part in the organization, we ended up at odds. She snuck a quick glance in my direction. "Do you still want to have sex?"

I was annoyed but not crazy. "Of course I do. The answer to that question is always a resounding yes."

Sariah giggled, straddling my lap. Claiming my chin, she angled my head until our eyes met. "Right now I'm just thinking out loud. I have no immediate plans to sell the team. And if and when I do decide I would appreciate your honest feedback."

"I just want to support you. I'm not trying to overstep."

"I appreciate your concern. But I can take care of myself. After all, I am Grover Thornton's daughter."

"Just be careful around Nolan. That's all." I got to rubbing on her thighs and any thoughts about the Ramblers, Nolan, or the future of the team dissipated.

SARIAH

With Justus away, I spent much of my time in New York. The Genuine Beauty skincare launch was now weeks away, not months and there was still so much to do. Currently, Tracie and I were in a Bronx warehouse inspecting the product packaging one final time.

"I love them. They look great," Tracie gushed.

I turned the container in my hand. "Are you sure? It looks more pink than lavender," I fretted. Picking up another bottle, I walked it to the window. In the light it was distinctly the lavender color we'd agreed on. "I guess it's fine."

"It has to be fine, the promotional boxes have already been shipped to celebrities and influencers."

"I know but this launch has to be perfect."

"And it will be. We still need to shore up the invites for the launch party. Is Justus coming?"

"Yes, I still have to ask him about the girls. It would mean they'd miss school the Friday of."

"Look at you. You're a stepmom." Tracie laughed at her words.

"Far from it."

"You're going shopping with those girls, flying back to Vegas to attend their volleyball games and packing school lunches. What do you call that?"

I shrugged. "What am I supposed to do, love on the man and ignore his kids?"

"No, I think all this is great. And I'm proud of you. Normally you would have run for the hills when you found out a man had kids."

"I know. But Justus is different." I smiled. "And before I knew what was happening, I was braiding hair, laying edges, and teaching them how to accomplish the perfect winged eyeliner."

"Justus is definitely one of a kind if he has you moving to Vegas. Which I'm not happy about."

"I'm not moving. I'm just going to be bi-coastal."

"Have you given any more thought to his offer to move into his place?" Tracie signed off on the packaging and handed the clipboard to me so I could do the same. One more item we could tick off our to do list.

"I'm still thinking about it. It just seems like a big step. And I know we're together all the time and it would make sense, but I like having a place of my own I can escape to when I need it."

"And he's okay with that?"

"He has to be. It doesn't mean I love him any less."

Her head jutted back. "Who are you and what have you done to my friend?"

"What do you mean?"

"You haven't used the L word when referring to a guy in years. You love pizza, you love pop up shops, you love our Drop Red Gorgeous lipstick. You do not love these hoes."

"Justus is only a hoe for me," I joked. "I've been ducking and dodging cupid for years. But somehow that chubby cherub still managed to shoot me center mass."

"Well, I can't wait for the wedding. And the babies," she cooed.

"Wedding? Maybe. Babies? Nah, get somebody else to do it."

"I need this to work. I'm living vicariously through your love life since mine is a series of unfortunate events."

"And I'm willing to give you the opulent wedding. But the runny nosed babies … are not on my vision board."

Tracie waved my words off, moving to another subject. "What time does your flight leave?"

"In a few hours." I was headed back to Vegas and back to Justus who was currently in the sky on his way home after a long two weeks on the road. Also, Nolan scheduled an urgent meeting for nine o'clock tomorrow morning and said it was imperative I be in attendance without offering any details as to the purpose of the meeting.

Much of the last two weeks I'd been MIA. I attended Rambler's meetings virtually, but my presence was needed in New York. Shit needed to get done that couldn't just be handed off to an assistant. The few times Nolan and I talked it was clear he was peeved about my absence. He even had the audacity to insinuate my father would be disappointed in my lack of interest.

When his words hit my ear, I was immediately turned off. I didn't work for Nolan, he worked for me and if I asked him to handle things while I was away, he damn sure better do it. Being berated and shamed because I was balancing multiple plates all spinning simultaneously was not helpful. Nolan Busch was rubbing me the wrong way and if he didn't fall in line, he could be replaced.

By the time I returned to Vegas, it was late and my reunion with Justus was less about words and more about our urgent need to physically connect. And connect we did. Thank God my headboard was cushioned because I would have suffered a concussion otherwise from the powerful thrust that made my knees weak and turned my core to jelly. His need for me was earnest and with little to no verbiage, he begged for the pussy, each stroke leaving me dripping wet for him. Talking could wait, right now all that mattered was his broad shoulders, strong arms, masterful tongue, and long dick.

I WAS DRAGGING FROM BOTH JET LAG AND THE DOUBLE header sex sessions with Justus, which didn't see my head hitting the pillow until well after two in the morning. When I entered the meeting room at the Ramblers' executive office it was a full house, in attendance was Nolan, Justus, and some other top executives. Justus's eyes seemed grave. He was blinking rapidly as if trying to communicate in morse code. Blink once for yes and twice for no. Also at the meeting was a representative from each of the minority shareholders. Most of whom I'd never personally met.

The contents of my stomach congealed. In the room, the air was heavy and other than Justus, no one else would meet my eyes. I'd learned to trust my instincts, it protected me both personally and professionally. My antenna was up and receiving the signal that this wasn't another boring budget meeting.

"Good morning. So many unfamiliar faces." I released a nervous laugh. Taking a seat at the head of the table, I waited expectantly.

"Shall we begin?" Nolan asked, not really looking for a response. "Sariah, so happy to have you back with us. We've missed your wise counsel these past few weeks."

Okay, this man was full of shit. I knew a damn dig when I heard one.

"Well as you know Nolan, I'm a busy woman. So let's not waste any time. Why are we all gathered here today?" Nolan called this meeting for a reason and the sooner we dispensed with the pleasantries and got to the point the better. But more importantly I wanted to know what this was all about so my heart could slow and stop rattling my chest.

"Good question. I called this meeting because I'm concerned. And quite frankly, I am not the only one who feels this way."

"What way?" There was a defiant tilt to my chin.

"Uncertain about the future of the organization that we all know and love. I'm not ashamed to say that for the first time in a long time I'm scared."

"Maybe you should see somebody about that." He couldn't be serious. Scared? Doubtful. Power hungry? Absofuckinglutely.

"For months now I've watched as you've tried to gather your bearings."

My head drew back in shock. "Gather my bearings?"

"It's no secret basketball and ownership of this team was thrust upon you. And if the past two weeks are any indication, this organization is not your priority."

"So you called this meeting to tell me you feel neglected?"

"I called this meeting to tell you the Ramblers won't play second fiddle to your beauty line endeavors. This is a billion-dollar organization and should be treated as such. There is no shame in admitting you're in over your head."

"Over my head?" My eyes darted to Justus practically pleading with him for some kind of clue as to where this was coming from. When he met my gaze, I could decipher his concern but what was missing was a sense of surprise. Why the fuck was Justus here? Did he agree with the idea I wasn't fit to lead? As Nolan continued to air his grievances, I examined the others in the room. All were stone faced, many shaking their heads emphatically whenever Nolan made a point they agreed with. They also all had one thing in common: they refused to look at me.

"Sariah we have waited patiently for you to get up to

speed but I'm afraid we have run out of time," Nolan said.

"Sounds ominous."

"It doesn't have to be." Nolan whispered to his assistant seated behind him and she quickly took off for the door. When she returned, she was accompanied by Derek Wayne.

"Good to see you again, Sariah." He had a huge Cheshire grin on his long face.

"Derek, what are you doing at a Ramblers' meeting?" This was a question I already knew the answer to. He was looking to buy a team and apparently Nolan informed him I had a team I was ready to offload.

Nolan was the one to answer my question. "We all appreciate how busy you are and it's clear this isn't working out for you or for us. By selling to Derek we all get what we want. We get a competent owner and you get to go back to New York and sit front row at fashion week."

This arrogant son of a bitch. This duplicitous asshole. My eyes settled on Justus once again. His jaw was rigid and he was cracking his knuckles. He appeared angry. *Was that anger directed at me? Was he unhappy with the direction the organization was moving in?* I hadn't even made a single change. *Maybe that's why he was upset.* In the five months I'd been owner I hadn't implemented any changes.

I cast my eyes around the conference table. "Does everyone in this room feel this way?"

"Trust me we are a united front," Nolan said.

Justus cleared his throat, but he didn't speak up. He

didn't defend me. I was standing in front of a firing squad and he was just going to let them execute me.

"Sariah, I understand wanting to honor your father's wishes, but you don't want to be here. And no one will blame you for walking away," Derek said in a pompous tone that vexed me upon our first meeting.

He was right. When I first inherited this team, I didn't want it. But these past months under Justus's tutelage and connecting with staff and players within the organization, my thinking had evolved. This team was my father's baby so much so he neglected his relationship with me for it. At the end of the day, I was still that girl trying desperately to make her father proud. The Ramblers offered me a chance to understand him better and maybe eventually even appreciate his sacrifices.

Derek placed a portfolio in front of me. Opening it, I skimmed the multiple pages, settling on the final document, an offer to purchase the team for one billion dollars. I took a deep cleansing breath, these motherfuckers thought I was dumb. It had been a long time since someone underestimated me. And Nolan and Derek's gross misrepresentation of me was like chucking gasoline soaked wood into a fire. One thing my father taught me was to never be reactive. Never operate out of a place of fear or anger. If I spoke up now, I would scorch the earth.

I looked at Justus one last time. *Was he here in support of me or Nolan? Did I just get played? Were Justus and Nolan working in tandem this whole time?*

Pushing back my chair, I said, "You've given me a lot

to think about. Thank you." Grabbing the portfolio with Derek's half ass offer, I exited the room headed to my office. Behind the closed door, I released a stuttering breath. *What just happened?* Of course, I understood some people weren't happy with the transition, but to gather in a room while their elected leader told me I wasn't shit and no one liked me was bizarre. And Justus, don't even get me started on Justus.

I texted Mr. Charles asking him to return to the office ASAP. Moving around the space, I instinctually collected items, my laptop, my tote bag, the picture frame on my desk of Tracie and me. Make no mistake, this was a retreat. My back was pressed against a wall, and I wasn't prepared to fight, so I had to flee via the nearest exit.

On my way out, I stopped at my assistant's desk. "Hi, can you please cancel my meetings for today."

"Of course, would you like me to reschedule them?"

"Nope … in fact cancel all my meetings."

"All?" Her smile flattened.

"Yep, if anyone asks, I'm out of the office indefinitely."

"Okay I will get right on it. What do you want me to tell anyone who request to schedule a future meeting?"

Tell them to go fuck themselves.

"Block my calendar and feel free to take the rest of the month off. On me, no need to use your vacation."

"Are you serious?"

"Yes, I'll call you when I need you again."

If Nolan and his crew didn't want me here, I'd act like a ghost and be gone. Outside, I paced the sidewalk, waiting for my ride. The realization setting in that it was highly probable Justus set me up. I don't know what Nolan offered him, maybe a contract extension or a hefty bonus, but I'd gotten duped.

As if on cue a deep voice called my name. "Sariah." Justus seemed frazzled and his limp was more pronounced than usual as he made his way over to me.

"What the actual fuck?" I practically spat out.

"That was a shit show."

"Yeah, and conveniently enough you had a front-row seat."

"Nolan texted me this morning and asked me to attend a last-minute meeting. I didn't know it was the same meeting you were going to."

"So you attended this impromptu meeting and just sat back and let Nolan eviscerate me?"

"What do you mean sat back?"

"I don't know." I lifted a sullen shoulder. "This whole time you've told me you support me and have my back. And the minute I needed you, you left me hanging."

The black SUV pulled up alongside us and Mr. Charles stepped out to open the passenger door, waiting in silence while Justus and I quarreled.

Justus squared his posture. "I've been trying to warn you about Nolan for months, but you didn't want to listen."

"So this shit is my fault?"

"That's not what I meant. Nolan was absolutely out of line."

I pinned my arms across my chest and examined his face for hidden subtext.

"Don't look at me like that."

"Like what?"

"Like you don't trust me." Justus grabbed hold of my face, maintaining shaky eye contact. "It's me Sariah, nothing has changed."

"Everyone in that meeting was against me."

"Not everyone. And for damn sure not me."

"Huh." I stepped back out of his reach. "But you just sat there and let them talk to me like that."

"Sariah, what did you want me to do? Chime in and then prove their point by undermining your leadership."

"I wanted you to support me." My composure was gone, and I was unable to keep my voice level. "I was alone in there and you just kept your head down."

"I'm sorry. I didn't want to make things worse."

Part of me wanted to melt into his arms and let him console me and the other part of me wanted to punch him in the gut. I needed to understand what role he played in all this. "Did you know Nolan was going to do this?"

His throat lurched with a hard swallow. "I didn't know this was going to happen today."

"But you knew it was going to happen?"

Justus displayed his palms in a form of surrender attempting to tamp down my reaction. "Sariah, I never expected—"

"I've heard everything I need to. Now run back to Nolan and Derek and have a great fucking laugh."

I climbed into the vehicle, ignoring Justus's pleas to explain. "When you're ready to talk—" The SUV drove away, leaving nothing but a shit ton of doubt between us.

I'd been in the workforce for a long time, and I'd encountered dirty business dealings. A peer stole a Genuine Beauty product idea. And a former employee left on what at the time seemed like amicable terms, but it was later discovered she stole our list of clients and contacts in hopes of enlisting them to work with her on her beauty line launch. That double cross ended in litigation. Running a business, especially as an entrepreneur, you were bound to get burned every now and again. But I never expected to get stabbed in the back by someone I trusted and loved.

JUSTUS

AFTER SARIAH LEFT ME IN A PLUME OF EXHAUST ON THE curb, I made my way back to the executive building. Getting to the suites was like trying to break into the gem room at the New York Museum of Natural History. Luckily for me I was friendly with the food staff. So when I knocked on the South entrance door, I was greeted by Clive who let me in with zero questions.

The freight elevator granted access to all floors, no escort required, and deposited me right where I wanted to be in front of Nolan's office suite. With determined strides, I bypassed his secretary, who was close on my heels, and entered unannounced.

"I'm sorry Mr. Busch. He wouldn't wait and insisted on seeing you," his secretary said.

"It's alright Jasmine. Please leave us alone." Nolan waved her away.

When the door closed behind her, I started in. "What the hell was that earlier?"

"Hello Coach Chappel it's good to see you again."

"Nolan. What the fuck?"

"Justus, please take a seat."

"I'm fine."

"Listen, sometimes you have to break a few eggs to make an omelet."

"That meeting was messy as fuck. Was that your version of an intervention?"

Nolan belted out a hearty laugh. "I like that, an owner intervention. God knows that woman needs it." He was relaxed and unbothered as if crushing people's spirit was a hobby.

"The last thing Sariah needed was to be accosted and demeaned."

"Consider it more of a wake-up call."

I was just as pissed at Nolan as I was at myself. Pissed for sitting in that meeting and letting the humiliation play out. Maybe Sariah was right … I should have spoken up. But I was legitimately torn. She didn't need me coming off as the knight riding in on some white horse. When people are questioning your leadership, you can't have others racing to your rescue. Basketball is all about strength and it was Sariah's responsibility to assert her power.

She literally held all the cards. Nolan and Derek could only offer idle threats because nothing would change ownership unless Sariah agreed to it. It was a stupid ploy to embarrass and shame her into submission. Busch thought he could bully ownership from her grasp, but all he'd done was make her clutch tighter. I didn't defend her at the meeting, but I was damn sure going to defend her now.

"What happened to gentle prodding?"

"She was moving too slow. I'd mentioned the possibility of selling and she'd listen and seem interested. And then the next time we talked she had a new set of reservations."

"Calling a meeting and demanding she sell was a horrible strategy."

"Well at least all the cards are laid out on the table. She knows we hate her and she'll get nothing but resistance if she retains ownership."

"We? You hate her for reasons I will never understand. If you look at the Ramblers' stats, our wins and losses, our ticket sales, and revenue, nothing has changed since Thornton's death. So why the rush to push her out?"

Nolan leaned forward, his jaw rigid and his shoulders square. "Because Grover gave that little girl what should have been mine. That lying bastard made promises he didn't keep."

I cocked a half-opened eye in his direction as I processed this new information. "Wait … what? Thornton promised you the Ramblers?"

"Yes, he said if anything ever happened to him the Ramblers would be mine."

"If that's the case, why are you pushing to have Derek Wayne buy it?"

Nolan's eyebrow scaled his forehead as he planted his arms over his chest.

My eyes sparked with comprehension. "Wait a minute. Derek isn't the sole buyer. You're in it too?"

"If the deal goes through, I'll be the majority owner with forty-five percent. Derek would own twenty percent. The other minority shareholders' stakes would remain unchanged."

"So this was never about Sariah or her leadership skills. This was always about you and your perceived slight at the hands of Grover Thornton."

"I worked my ass off for that man and this organization. Long nights, missed time with my family. When my daughter got married four years ago I was on the phone negotiating the Perkins trade. I missed the father and daughter dance. I deserve what I'm owed."

"Sounds like you worked your fingers to the bone for a man who didn't give a fuck about you. It happens, we've all been there. But to assume you have a greater claim to this team than Sariah is laughable."

Who hadn't worked overtime, pitched thoughtful ideas, or missed out on precious time with family or friends, all in the hopes of landing a promotion? A promotion that never came or was awarded to someone else. It all made sense now. Nolan was a bitter old man who sunk everything into this organization. And even though he was compensated handsomely for it, it still wasn't enough.

Poor entitled bastard.

"And publicly humiliating her was what … an added bonus?"

"Justus you and I both know that woman is in the weeds without a compass."

"I disagree. Sariah is a smart and shrewd businesswoman. And if you'd taken the opportunity to really get to know her you would've learned she's dedicated to this team and our players."

"So you're the authority on Sariah Thornton now?"

"Why did you have to drag me into your vendetta? You could've missed me with all this bullshit. I didn't need to be at the fucking meeting."

"I just wanted her to know she has no allies. That everyone is against her," he said smugly.

My hands balled into tight fists. I wanted to jump over the desk and pummel him in the face. This resentful prick wanted to hurt Sariah and he used me as a pawn to do it. She may never talk to me again, but he'd gotten his lick back, so it was all good.

"You egotistical asshole. The Ramblers aren't yours and they never will be. If I have anything to say about it."

Nolan stood in an attempt to assert his power. "You do know I could fire you?" For authority to be effective, you had to be respected. His idle threats fell on deaf ears.

"You can't do shit. You don't own this fucking team."

"It's just a matter of time. And when I get the call that Sariah's signed the contract my next call will be to relieve you of your coaching duties."

"Did you ever stop to ask yourself why Thornton didn't leave you the team like he promised? I think it's because he recognized you were a sniveling little bitch." I turned and exited his office, and a satisfied smirk took over my face.

"You called Nolan a sniveling bitch?" Deck asked in partial shock.

"Yeah, and it felt good. Hella good."

After the fall out from Nolan's smash and grab meeting, I'd planned to stay mum on what transpired. But word traveled fast and rumors, mostly false, were floating around the facility. I'd heard it all ... Sariah left the room in tears, that she lunged at Nolan and had to be removed from the building by security. Some were saying Nolan was only doing what Grover would've wanted. People were choosing sides with zero facts. I finally broke down and called Deck, ready to vent. Never one to miss out on gossip, he invited me over.

"You do know when he gets the chance he will toss you out on your ass, right?"

"Yeah, well I'm sure Sariah is having her legal team draft up my severance package as we speak." I took a long gulp of ice tea.

"So still no word from her?"

"She said she needed time to think. But it's been a week. When I called her assistant's desk, I got some generic message about Sariah being out of office and if you need immediate assistance, you should call some random one eight hundred number."

"That's tough. Do you think Nolan broke her and she just said fuck it and walked away?"

"She's pissed but she's not a quitter."

Deck gestured at a cheese and meat board.

"Did you put this together?"

"Fuck no. You know Raphael be out here making

shit. He threw this together, called it an all day grazing board."

"It's impressive. I know some rich folks that would pay top dollar for shit like this."

"Well keep that to yourself. I'm not trying to fund any more entrepreneurial endeavors." Deck tossed a cheese cube in his mouth. "What are you going to do about Sariah?"

"What can I do? I want to be respectful and give her time to process what happened, but I don't want her thinking I'm a traitor."

It pained me to imagine what she must think of me right now. She probably thought every word I ever uttered was a lie. And that the sex was just a perk while I waited for Nolan and Derek to shake her down. I wrote a long pathetic text message but then decided not to send it. Any explanation needed to occur in person, a text message couldn't convey the nuance of this situation.

"I'm sure she'll come around. In the meantime, if Nolan tries to be slick and fire you he'll have a mini rebellion on his hands."

"That's the thing. Sariah thinks everyone is against her. But I've talked to some of the other people who attended that meeting, and they were just as shocked at the direction of that conversation as she was. Nolan claims his beliefs are widely shared within the organization but that's just another one of his lies."

"I'm certainly not team Nolan."

"I just wish there was a way to knock him down a few pegs."

"Everyone has skeletons in their closet, maybe it's time to bust open a few doors."

"Flip the script." I tapped my temple in appreciation of his suggestion.

"Now I'm not advocating revenge. But it's hard to move on when shit isn't square."

"I'm damn sure going to need things to be even stevens before this is all through." I flexed my right leg under the table.

Deck critically scanned my movements. "Have you made a decision about knee surgery yet?"

"Actually, I have. After talking with Sariah and some of Dr. Samuelson's former patients, I've decided to move forward with the surgery."

"I'm glad to hear it."

"It took me a minute, but I finally came around. I scheduled the procedure for the off season so I'll have time to fully recover."

"And when you wake up you'll be surrounded by smiling faces. The girls, me, Sariah."

I shot him a look at the mention of Sariah.

"Okay, maybe not Sariah but me and the girls for sure."

Thanks man I appreciate it and you for listening to me."

"Remember my friend, the thing is not the thing. It's the thing you *think* about the thing."

"Uhm … okay."

"Yeah, Sloane and I have been listening to this self-help book about recognizing your worth and not letting people or situations undervalue you. Not going to lie it's blown my mind a few times. The best thing about you is you." Deck smirked.

I stretched my eyes wide. Deck never ceased to surprise me. "It sounds kind of granola."

"It's granola as fuck but it's helping me and Sloane work through some of our shit from childhood. We want to be better people for Destiny, Ace, and the baby."

"Lil Justus or Justina will appreciate that," I joked.

SARIAH

Mini golf was a silly game, but I needed silly and lighthearted shit to take my mind off the descent into hell my life had taken. Tracie was my bestest friend but when it came to competitive activities, we had a fierce rivalry. I was currently trying to get my ball through the mouth of a huge rattlesnake. Its tail shook to produce a grating buzzing noise every time I attempted to strike the ball.

When I finally hit the ball and it coasted down the throat of that reptile, I performed a twerking dance I quickly realized was inappropriate for a Saturday afternoon at the family friendly venue. At the end of the course, Tracie bested me to my great dismay. We headed to the food counter for spiked lemonades before finding a table outside.

"I should bring Zander here. I think he'd like it."

"So you and baby brother Zander are still going strong?"

"Yes, I'm doing my best to make time for him at least once a month. A few weeks ago, we went to the aquarium. He's a good kid. Smart and funny. And when I look at him, he reminds me of Benji. Truthfully seeing traces of Benji in his personality hurt initially but now I weirdly find it comforting."

"You really are turning into an old softy in your advanced age."

I cackled. "Advanced age? You do realize you're two years older than me."

"Yes, so that makes me an authority on the terrain."

I rolled my eyes taking a sip of the slushed lemonade. Flipping over the scorecard I was still trying to figure out how she managed to beat me. "You got lucky today. You won't catch me slipping again."

"Sariah?"

"Hmm," I said absentmindedly while recounting the tally.

"Don't you think you should give Justus a chance to explain?" Tracie's words caught me off guard. Since picking her up from the airport yesterday, we hadn't mentioned Justus and I was hoping we could keep it that way. I asked Tracie to come to Vegas because I needed a distraction even if it was only for twenty-four hours.

"And when his explanation is bullshit … then what?" I tossed the scorecard aside as disdain settled over my face.

"You owe him an opportunity to say his piece. Maybe you two can salvage this."

"He's literally the modern-day Judas betraying me for twelve pieces of silver."

Tracie expelled a long breath. "Do you know for a fact he betrayed you?"

"He was in that meeting with everyone else just watching while Nolan talked to me like I was a child."

"Maybe he was blindsided just like you were."

"Or maybe he's just a liar out for himself."

Tracie fidgeted with her bottom lip, which she often did when she wanted to say something but was uncertain how I would take it.

"Just say whatever it is you're thinking."

"I hate to bring this up but remember a few months back when your father wanted to talk to you and you wouldn't return his calls or answer his text messages."

My eyes slammed into hers. "This isn't the same."

"When people hurt you, you shut down and X them from your life. And sometimes I fear you walk away from people without ever getting the full story. You're unable to see past your feelings." Tracie raised her palms. "You have every right to feel what you feel. But I'm not always sure your feelings are rooted in the truth."

I pinned my arms over my chest. I wasn't used to Tracie not taking my side.

"You were happy with Justus and talking about moving in together and then one little thing—"

"Major thing. I consider duplicity a major thing."

"Sariah we are grown and healing and that means we have the tough conversations even if in the end we ultimately have to cut ties. Avoiding him isn't going to make it hurt any less."

She sounded like my therapist. Who also advised me to close the loop with Justus.

"I don't think you understand how deeply he hurt me."

"Love comes with a hearty serving of vulnerability on the side. You can't have one without the other." Tracie fluffed her voluminous curls. "Did you ever read your father's letter?"

"Yes of course I did." I couldn't meet her eyes because then she'd see I was lying.

"Lying to me isn't going to make it true."

Correction, apparently Tracie didn't need to look at me to detect a lie.

"I'm going to read the letter."

"When?"

"Damnit Tracie can you just give it all a rest? I don't want to talk about Justus or my father. Thank you very much."

"Well excuse the fuck outta me." She pressed her lips into a straight line, turning away from me to witness the water spiking from the nearby fountain.

I scooched over, wrapping my arms around her. "Tracie," I called out in a sing-song tone. "I'm sorry I know you're only trying to help. I'm not mad at you. I'm just deep in my feelings but that doesn't give me the right to take it out on you."

Tracie angled her body toward me, returning my hug. "I just want you to be good, you fucking doofus."

"I know and I love you for it."

After a quick bite to eat, I dropped Tracie off at McCarran and we said our goodbyes with extended hugs and fits of giggles, like I wouldn't see her again in a few days. Back at my apartment, I took a long hot bath and decided to entertain myself with a movie. A messy drama was in order. Watching someone else's chaotic life would definitely distract me from the problems in my own.

Ruffling the sheets, I hoped the remote would tumble out from the folds. Next, I padded toward the nightstand, opening the drawer, which was filled with takeout menus, empty gum wrappers, random Post-it notes, and my father's letter. That letter made it from the bottom of my purse, to the bedroom end table and finally the drawer of that table when I was tired of looking at it.

Everyone told me to read it and I agreed I needed to open the damn letter, but each time I tried, I'd find five other tasks that suddenly demanded my attention. One afternoon was spent reorganizing my closet from hats to shoes. At the end of the decluttering session, I made a hollow promise I'd read it tomorrow or the next day.

Ripping the sealed envelope, I pulled the pages from it.

Sariah,

If you're reading this then regretfully, I'm dead. Unfortunately, regret is the running theme in my life. I'm hopeful this letter is finding you in a better place than I am. I've sat down and attempted to capture these words on paper on many occasions. Harper is the one who suggested I do this and since you're not currently speaking to me it seemed like a good idea.

I'm sorry for the way our last conversation went. You said some things that caught me by surprise. Maybe that's the problem, your old man is totally oblivious to how you really feel about me and our relationship. You were right when Benji died, I changed but not for the reasons you think.

I decided the best way to deal with the pain was with distance. So I separated myself from you and your mother. With the hope that it wouldn't hurt as bad if I ever lost you. When you were born, I'd never experienced that type of love in all my life. I held your tiny body in the palm of my hand. You were so small and fragile. I was afraid if I breathed too hard I'd bruise you. But in the moment, sitting next to your mother in the hospital room I knew my life would never be the same because in the palm of my hand I was holding my whole world and the living embodiment of my heart. And when we had Benjamin it happened again.

Losing your brother destroyed me. I loved him with my entire being. And I didn't want to hurt like that ever again, so I inserted a wedge between us. While I thought I was protecting my heart I was really just slowly tearing it to shreds. I know now that choice was the wrong one. And I'm reminded of that fact every time I look into your eyes. I see the hurt and disappointment ... it's written all over your face.

Let me use this opportunity to say what I should have said years ago. I don't blame you for Benji's death. I was just so relieved I didn't lose you both. I don't secretly wish you were the child that died that day. The fact that you think I could ever wish it hurts my heart. I've always loved you even though I did a piss poor job of showing it. I fucked up and made you hate me. And I know when I take my last breath that will be my biggest regret. All the time missed, all the conversations that dissolved into arguments. All the words left unsaid.

Not a day passes where I'm not proud of you. The way

you started your own business with no help from your dad. Genuine Beauty is your baby and you should be proud of it. I have my assistant search for news articles and social media posts about you so I can review them each night. News about you is sort of my bedtime story because it provides so much comfort.

Now that I'm gone I ask that you look after Zander. He could benefit from having you in his life. I know you're not a fan of Harper but she's actually not that bad once you get to know her. Zander's your brother so please don't push him away to spite me. I think you'll find him to be bright and curious and sometimes when I look at him I swear it's like Benji is working through him.

Finally, the will. I left you gotdamn nearly everything because you are my precious baby girl. And a savvy business woman. I don't care what you do with your inheritance. Shit sell it all off if you want to. What is most important to me is that you're taken care of and happy.

I've been very fortunate and yet I still squandered away happiness. I want better for you.

I'm sorry I sucked at being a dad. I hoped to do a better job with Zander. You know right some of my mistakes. Hopefully it's enough. Maybe if we're lucky I can say this stuff to you in person the next time we're together.

Well that's it kiddo. I love you more than life itself which is funny seeing how I'm most likely dead.

Take care of yourself, Jellybean.

Love Dad.

The pages were damp from my endless tears. Deep sobs that coursed through my body and raced down my cheeks. No longer upright, I'd dissolved into a crumpled heap on the floor. My wails bounced off the walls, the mournful echoes assaulting my ears. The letter mentioned unsaid words ... my tears were for all the words I never got the chance to say. He wasn't the only one with regrets. I was drowning in them. My chin trembled and my incessant weeping would not let up.

These tears were coming from a well of emotions rarely tapped. Pain that had been held captive for far too long was finally being freed. During my therapy sessions, Dr. Ang was working with me to communicate the hurt I felt. Each time she did, she was met with my resistance. Because I feared this precise moment, this ugly cry overtook my spirit, leaving my chest excruciatingly tight and my stomach in binding knots.

It took me an hour to stop balling and another thirty minutes to wrangle in the wayward tears. When I finally peeled myself off the plush carpet, I reached for my phone. No more unarticulated words. Failing to have a conversation robbed me of a real relationship with my father, I refused to let it happen again.

Sariah: Do you still want to talk?

Justus: Desperately.

Sariah: I could come to you or you could swing this way.

Justus: It's late. I'll come to you. Give me forty-five minutes.

Sariah: See you then.

JUSTUS

In the elevator of the Waldorf, I rehearsed what I would say. I'd tell her I was sorry. No excuses, no defense, just a sincere apology. After I'd explain exactly how I got pulled into this mess of a situation. Then to round it out, I'd offer up a bit of begging for forgiveness with earnest vows to never make her question my loyalty again.

I stood at her front door far too long, fidgeting with my shirt and checking my breath, which was still minty fresh. Finally, I gave the door a timid knock and waited. Nerves danced in my stomach. I didn't like being in "trouble." Even as a kid I was a model student who followed all the rules. Typically, if I was at odds with somebody, it was their fault because I went out of my way to see the best in people. The realization I was to blame for Sariah's mistrust was a hard pill to swallow.

When she opened the door, she didn't say hello or offer a welcoming smile … Sariah immediately started the interrogation. "Were you working with Nolan to sabotage me?"

"No, of course not."

Being apart, I'd forgotten just how beautiful she really was. Effortlessly fine in a T-shirt and lounge pants. Satisfied with my response, she stepped aside, allowing me to pass over the threshold. The fragrance of her skin triggered a desire to cuff her by the neck and ask for the green light to fuck her until she accepted my apology.

"Tell me there's a perfectly sane explanation that doesn't involve you repeatedly stabbing me in the back?"

"Listen I fucked up. And I should've brought this shit to your attention sooner but I'm not in cahoots with Nolan Busch or Derek Wayne." I shook my head at the absurdity of it all.

Sariah pointed me toward the couch. Half-eaten Chinese takeout was spread out on the coffee table. "Okay, start from the beginning. How did this happen?" she asked, reaching for her almost empty mixed drink.

I wasted no time catching her up. For this to work there couldn't be any more secrets between us. "Nolan approached me shortly after you inherited the team. He basically said he didn't think you were a good fit and he was going to try to convince you to sell to Derek Wayne."

Any hint at her happiness to see me had faded, and Sariah was now all business. "Was this before we started dating?"

"Yes."

"And how did you respond?"

"I just kind of shrugged it off. I thought it was talk

that would lead to nowhere." I fed a long, pan-fried noodle into my mouth.

"Did he ask you to choose sides?"

"No, honestly he just assumed I was in his corner from the beginning."

"Is that because you allowed him to think that?" Sariah's brows climbed her forehead. Her expression forced me to realize that even though we'd spent months getting to know one another and experienced nights filled with leg quivering, soul snatching, dick pulsating sex, she wasn't going to go easy on me.

"I told him on more than one occasion there was no way you were going to sell. Could I have been clearer about where I stood? Yes. But he definitely knows how I feel now."

"What do you mean?"

"After the meeting I gave Nolan a piece of my mind. It didn't end well. He threatened to fire me."

"Maybe I should let him." She stuck her chopsticks in a half empty container of Ma Po Tofu.

Pulling my face into a frown, I said, "Ouch."

"I've been pissed and thoughts of firing you and Nolan kind of helped me fall asleep at night."

"You thought I'd set you up so I can't blame you for wanting to even the score."

"Why didn't you tell me?" Her tone was agitated.

"I tried to warn you several times that Nolan didn't have your best interest at heart, but you didn't really want to listen."

"You said that same shit after the meeting. But if you'd told me Nolan was trying to steal the organization from under me, maybe I'd have been a little more receptive."

My shoulders slumped. "I should've taken it more seriously. Even after we met with Derek I didn't expect for Nolan to pull that meeting stunt."

Sariah gasped and her eyes were feral. "You met with Derek Wayne about buying my team?"

Had I failed to mention this before? "Nolan invited me to a meeting. When I got there Derek showed up and they started talking about their evil plan."

"So I'm going to ask you again. Why didn't you tell me?"

"Because the plan was stupid. You have majority control and nothing shakes unless you sign off on it. You can't be voted out. They have no leverage, no power. It's all just smoke and mirrors. They're using intimidation and fear tactics to try and run you off."

Sariah's body sunk into the couch, releasing some of the uneasiness that was wedged between us.

"I didn't want to step on your toes, or influence your decision to keep or sell the team. My focus was on trying to support you. Maybe I should've rode harder for you. But this sport demands leadership. Me shielding you from the realities of this business would not have been beneficial. When you hired me as your tutor it was always my goal to provide you with the tools and resources to navigate the league even if I wasn't there.

"I'm sorry I thought not helping you was helping you. If that makes sense. I just wanted you to recognize you're more than capable of standing ten toes down and making tough decisions. I should've told you about Nolan and Derek. You just had so many other things vying for your attention and I didn't want to add to that stress."

"I don't think you understand how alone I felt in that meeting, Justus. Some of those people were smiling in my face and offering their support just a few weeks ago. And somehow Nolan turned them all against me. No one would look at me. You were supposed to be my ally."

"I am your ally."

"Allies support one another. Allies don't sit back in silence while you're getting jumped by a gang. Nolan belittled me and my experience in front of everybody and you didn't even bat an eye."

"I didn't want to exacerbate an intense situation."

"It was already pretty bad. I don't think you choosing to speak on my behalf would've made much of a difference to them. But for me … I was searching for a lifeline and hoped you'd be my rip cord before I hit the ground."

I reached for her, clasping her hands in mine. "I made the wrong call. I thought speaking up would undermine your authority. Which is the last thing I ever want to do. People remember shit like that. And then next thing you know it's comments about your inability to fight your own battles. The way people perceive you as an owner is important. And it's a delicate balance. Once a person starts thinking of you as weak it's hard to unring that bell."

Sariah's head snapped back. "Do you think I'm weak?"

"I think you're akin to some type of supernatural being. Not many people could manage all the irons you have burning in the fire. I fell in love with you because you're resilient and smart as a whip, and you have a passion to succeed. You also had the foresight to hire me to help you do that. I know there is nothing you can't do because I've seen you accomplish so much. Running Genuine Beauty and prepping for the upcoming launch, not to mention the other shit you inherited. Managing all that while building a relationship with your baby brother and making time in your life for my kids."

"I just don't want to fuck this up," she whispered.

I kissed the inside of her wrist. "You can't. I won't let you."

"You sound like my father in his letter to me."

"So you finally read it?"

"I did."

"Good for you."

She nodded. "He believed in me." Her eyes misted over with tears.

"He's not the only one who believes in you, Sariah."

Her gaze pinged over my features as if analyzing the veracity of my words. When she was done measuring the truthfulness of my claims, her gaze slowly slipped to the crotch of my sweatpants and my dick swelled with desire for her, making it visible through the fabric. Sariah's nipples pebbled, pushing against her lightweight T-shirt.

"Maybe I overreacted. According to Tracie I'm quick

at cutting people off under the pretense of protecting my peace. I'm sorry I doubted you."

I cupped her face, stroking her cheek with my thumb. Sariah's body was no longer tightly drawn as she leaned into my palm.

"And I'm sorry I gave you a reason to doubt."

I sunk my face into her hair, which was natural and curly, denoting she'd likely washed it since this morning and hadn't gotten around to straightening it. Finding her ear underneath the mass of curls I whispered, "This week has been rough without you. I missed us."

Her sultry eyes met mine and silently begged me to dick her down. I pulled her from the couch guiding her to the dining table. Sariah was already pulling off her fluffy lounge pants. To my delight she wasn't wearing any underwear. Pulling out the nearest chair, I took a seat and feasted on her ass while she worked her clit. Her anus received gentle attention before my tongue dipped inside, synchronized with the cadence of her moans and grunts.

I missed Sariah for a multitude of reasons, and these past few days I stressed over the possibility of never making her laugh again or breathing in her scent as I fell asleep. Never experiencing the tickle in my belly when she reached for my hand. Or the sensation of her nails scratching my back after a long day. Losing moments like this, in which her eyes were hooded and focused solely on me. It was just me and her and our rapacious desire to become one.

I reveled as she fingered herself inches from my face while I stroked my dick. Sariah was spread out like a banquet ... legs wide, breast jiggling, working her clit until it was plump and wet. Standing, I stripped down to my birthday suit and I slid my penis along her slit before centering my tip against her bud. She clawed at the table while I teased her with the head of my dick.

Encouraging her to sit up, I gave my dick a wag. One side of her mouth curved into a grin before slipping her wet fingers into my mouth so I could lick them clean. When her lips settled around my penis, I seeped in air. The muscles in my abdomen flexed with a twitch. My eyes grew wide as she worked her way up my shaft, making it disappear. The sounds of her softly gagging while easing me further down her throat enraptured me.

I collected her mass of curls, using it as a helm to help her suck while I rocked my hips. A week hadn't been the longest we'd gone without sex, but being without her these past eight days made me all the more ravenous as if I was attempting to make up for the lost time. Her tongue curled around my dick, making it pulsate in her mouth. Pulling out, I descended on her lips with appreciative kisses, thanking her for the skillful tongue game. I was greedy for her, latching on to her mouth with messy gluttonous kisses. Standing tall, I fed her my dick and watched with a carnal gaze at the tongue to tip action. Ribbons of arousal unraveling in my core. Quickly pulling away, I did my best to tamper down the impending release that threatened to wash over me.

Dropping to my knees, I returned the favor, licking and suckling until her body retreated, inching away from the onslaught of her orgasm. I hooked my arms over her legs, sucking until she convulsed and called on the heavens. When her body settled, I resumed with slow methodical circles that twirled over the surface of her pussy before diving deep. In short order, she was once again in a frenzied state as a second wave crashed over her. She deserved a proper apology, and multiple orgasms seemed like fair compensation.

Scooping her off the dining table, I carried her to the bedroom. I deposited her face down and gently smacked her ass until she was on all fours and level with my crotch. Running my tip over her slit, I slowly inched myself inside. Sariah's body softened into the mattress and after a few well-timed thrusts, her speech was muddled. I slapped her ass harder this time and with my hand braced around her neck, I pulled her back on all fours.

"Can you tell how much I missed you?"

She flashed me a steel gaze. "Yes, I feel it."

"Don't … ever … take … my … pussy … away." I punctuated each word with a thrust that momentarily snatched the air from her lungs.

When she finally regained the capacity to speak, she begged me for more. I planted my face in between her legs, taking decadent sips of her essence. Her high-pitched cries tickled me. Lowering myself to the bed, I slipped back inside with ease. Sariah's core molded snuggly around my dick as she worked her hips in time with mine.

Do you know how rare it is to find someone who gets you? Sariah and I were cut from the same cloth. We had matching work ethics and we're both passionate about our careers and the people we loved. I'd been single a long time and accepted that the bar was in hell and the chances of me finding someone who lit my soul on fire was unlikely. I normally wasn't a territorial person, but Sariah was mine. God entrusted her heart to me. And my new directive was to make her feel loved, nurtured, and supported.

"I'm gonna come," Sariah managed to eek out.

Kissing her forehead, I directed her, "Let it all out baby. Give me all that fucking energy." Her body shivered and primal screams underscored the moment. Sariah's satisfaction spurred on my own. Tensing, I hugged her close and showered her with every ounce of my love.

After our heart rates slowed and I snuck in a few more kisses, we lay exhausted but satisfied in each other's arms. Sariah's hand swept over my chest. "He can't get away with this."

"Who … Nolan?"

"Yeah, how do we stick it to the bastard?"

"I have a few ideas if you want to hear them."

"Operation take Nolan Busch down is in full effect," she chimed before planting a kiss to my lips to seal the deal.

SARIAH

For the next few weeks Justus and I brainstormed the most effective way to take Nolan down. I mean, sure I could just fire him. But I was a petty bitch, so I wanted to humiliate him and then fire him. It was late on a Friday when Justus's phone chimed. As he read the incoming message, a smile crept over his face.

"What is the smirk about?"

"I think I just may have been handed a smoking gun."

"Please do share with the class," I said, snagging another street taco from the platter."

"After the power play by Nolan and Derek I decided to do some digging."

"Into?"

"Everything, financials, potential mistresses, a secret love child."

"Are you telling me Nolan has a secret love child?"

"No."

I snapped my fingers at the missed opportunity. "Darn."

"What he does have is a shit ton of debt. Bad investments, outstanding loans. He is leveraged up the wazoo."

"Okay so how does that help us? Clearly, he was able to secure the funds for the potential team purchase."

"The one thing Nolan prides himself on is appearances. What people think of him is important. And if it got out that he was essentially a beggar it would impact his pride and change the way people view him."

"It could also spur Derek Wayne to walk away." Does he really want to align himself with someone who could file for bankruptcy in a few years?" Searching for my pad of paper, I was prepared to jot down some notes.

"Or even worse someone who's dire need for an infusion of cash could lead to him raiding the coffers."

"Wait, do you mean stealing money?"

"Yeah. Lance from accounting once told me about a time a few years back when the Ramblers' financial numbers were off. Money was moved or some shit. At the time he couldn't share all the details but he insinuated Nolan was behind it. I didn't think much of it back then, just company gossip."

"Get the fuck outta here."

"Hand to the Bible. They couldn't prove it but there were some distinct pieces of evidence that pointed to an inside job and Nolan was the likely suspect. Lance just emailed over some of the documents that incited the alarm."

"And my dad just let that shit slide?"

"Apparently, this information was never disclosed to

Thornton. Nolan ended up firing some second level executive and claimed the problem was resolved."

"Do you think he could still be stealing money?"

"It's possible. He damn sure has a need for funds."

My face lit up. "Are you thinking what I'm thinking?"

"I was thinking about having some more chips and salsa so probably not."

"I should have my accountants review the documents from Lance and the organizations financial records independent of the internal Ramblers accounting team."

"You haven't already done that?"

"No. The Ramblers had a fully staffed accounting unit. Why would I pay someone else to perform the job they were already doing?"

Grabbing my phone, I shot off an email to my accountant. I wanted a full external audit of the Ramblers' organization's books. With a special focus on the dates of strange activity listed in the documents Lance shared. And I needed it done yesterday. Within minutes I received a reply. One of the perks of having a billion dollars in your bank account was expedited response times. Jeffery assured me he could pull a team together and start the audit process by Monday.

With the information Justus provided and my top-notch accounting firm, Nolan's days with the Ramblers were numbered.

As much as I wanted Justus in the meeting with me, this was something I had to handle on my own. I'd summoned Nolan to my office so I had the upper hand. Weeks had passed since his ambush which left me reeling. This was actually my first time stepping foot into the executive office since that day. As I made my way through the halls, heads turned and whispers followed.

No bitches, I wasn't under a rock crying my eyes out. I mean I certainly went through a funk that consisted of "woe is me" energy and triple chocolate ricotta ice cream, but I was ready to reclaim my power. When my assistant opened the door leading Nolan in, I stood from my desk, squaring my shoulders. Before the door was fully closed behind him, Nolan launched into a speech that was far more confident than he had a right to be.

"Sariah, my dear. Good to see you again. I hope you've spent the last few weeks considering Derek's offer."

"I have been very busy these past few weeks. It's been a fruitful time. Please have a seat." I motioned toward the set of chairs on the other side of my desk.

"We like fruitful missions. I'm sure your legal team informed you the offer is a generous one."

"So what are you ... acting as Derek Wayne's intermediary?"

"Derek is a busy man and he trusts me to get this done."

"Hmm, it's a shame he'll ultimately end up disappointed."

"In what way?" He propped his left leg on his knee.

"In your ideal of guidance."

"I never led you astray."

"No, you just purposely hid your motives. You wanted me to sell the Ramblers from the moment I walked through those glass doors."

"I was looking out for the best interest of the team."

"I think you and I both know you are most concerned about your own welfare."

"What are you going on about?"

"When Derek Wayne made his *generous* offer, I decided to look into the organization's finances. I wanted to make an informed decision." I rested my elbow on the desk, leaning forward. "Do you want to venture a guess at what I found?"

Nolan appeared to look inward at his black soul before once again focusing on me. "With all due respect, I'm not interested in playing games."

"Unless it's the shell game … right? Swipe a hundred thousand and make it disappear. What's a few thousand dollars to an organization making millions?"

"Excuse me?"

"But you didn't stop at the first one hundred thousand. You got greedy and over the course of the last five years you secretly siphoned away millions of dollars. Two million seven hundred and eighty thousand to be precise."

"I would choose your next words very carefully little girl. I know you're upset but I will not tolerate false accusations."

Discreetly, I pressed a button on my desktop phone. "Thief. You're a thief, Nolan. You've been stealing money from the charitable works arm of the Ramblers' organization for years." My office door opened and two security personnel entered and stationed themselves nearby.

Nolan released a dark laugh. "You have no respect for your elders. I built this organization."

"My father did."

"I did, he just took all the credit. I'm the one that poured over hundreds of hours of footage. I'm the one that aggressively recruited Colin Pratt and Deion McCabe. It was the implementation of my vision that will have us in the finals if not this year then next year."

I folded my arms on the desk. "Thank you for your dedication but going forward your services are no longer needed."

Nolan choked on his words. "Are you firing me?"

"Yes. I'm firing you. My legal team will be speaking with law enforcement. Your Ramblers pension will be forfeited due to theft and dishonesty. You said the organization needed to change. I'm just giving you what you wanted."

Smoke was practically steaming out of his ears. "You can't do this. You have no right."

"See where I come from, we have a saying, fuck around and find out. You decided to fuck around by trying to push me out of my company. And now ... well now you're finding out I was never the one to cross fake on."

"You fucking bitch." His lips were quivering, and beads of sweat coasted down his face. I imagine he was fighting the urge to jump across the oak desk and choke me out.

"My name is Sariah and I'm Grover Thornton's daughter. If you don't know now you do." The security guards advance forward to help Nolan out of the building.

Nolan stood, buttoning his suit jacket in an attempt to gather some semblance of respectability. "You are making a big mistake."

I wrinkled my nose. "Hmm … I disagree." I couldn't hide the twinkle in my eye as he exited my office, followed closely behind by security.

I think my father would be proud. He'd missed Nolan's double dealing and theft because he trusted him. It felt good being able to right this wrong. Grover Thornton was never one to give people multiple chances and if he knew what I knew, his actions would have mirrored mine. Knowing my father, the police would be carting Nolan away to a jail cell and not just off the premises. My legal team would handle any pending litigation. I was just glad to get rid of the two-faced traitor.

After Nolan's walk of shame, I went in search of Justus, finding him shooting a ball around on one of the smaller practice courts in his suit and dress shoes. Once he caught sight of me, he released the ball meeting me at center court, concern marred his face. "How'd it go?"

"Nolan has been escorted off the property, his company phone and tablet were confiscated. And his personal belongings will be shipped to his home."

"God I would've loved to see the look on his face."

"He kind of looked like this." I imitated a dumbstruck expression. "He underestimated the wrong woman."

"What about criminal charges?"

"That's still on the table. I gave my lawyers the green light to turn over the audit findings to the police."

"Damn. Nolan should have just fallen in line. Now he's out of a job and facing jail time."

"Life comes at you fast." We indulged in a much-needed moment of levity. "Thank you for being there for me."

"I'm kind of in love with you so it goes with the territory."

"Kind of?"

"Okay, insanely in love with you is more accurate." He reached for my hand, giving it a tender squeeze.

Justus really had become my rock. I'd been solo dolo for so long I'd forgotten what it felt like to have a shoulder to lean on, a hand to hold, and a thick dick to ride. He'd patiently answered all my basketball questions as we watched hours of footage. The job of tutor was one he took seriously transferring his wealth of knowledge about the game and the business down to me. All of which played a part in empowering me to stand up to Nolan. He wasn't just my lover, he was also my best friend. And there was no one else I wanted by my side.

A thought formed in my head. "Would you be interested in the general manager position?"

"As much as I appreciate the offer. I think you should meet with potential candidates and determine who best aligns with your vision for this team."

"So was that a no? Because the job is yours if you want it."

"It's not a no. I just really want to bring the team to a championship. That's important to me. Maybe in a few years we can revisit this conversation."

"I'm going to hold you to that." I caressed his cheek softly tugging at his whiskers. "One last favor?"

"Anything."

"I need you to take a trip with me to Kansas to recruit Aldridge Mosley. I've had several meetings with him already."

Justus jerked his head back, an incredulous expression taking over his features. "Why didn't you say anything?"

"Because I didn't want to get your hopes up. But now I need you to talk to him coach to player and close this deal."

"I can do that." He tossed his arm over my shoulder. "We make a great team."

"I'm the brains, you're the beauty," I teased.

"So partner, what do you want to do next?" he asked, planting a quick kiss to my lips.

I kicked off my heels. "Teach me how to play basketball."

"Really?"

"Yep, I told you I wanted to learn everything."

Justus reclaimed possession of the ball. "Okay it all starts with a jump ball."

"Jump ball, got it."

He hoisted the ball over our head. "Eyes on the ball. Ready?"

"Ready Coach."

"One, two, three …"

JUSTUS

EPILOGUE

I WAS A FEW WEEKS OUT FROM MY SURGERY, BUT IT WOULD take a lot more than hobbling with the assistance of a cane to keep me from Sariah's skincare launch. Today was important to her, so Ebony, Jhené, and I flew to New York via one of Sariah's corporate plane. The private jet made the five-hour flight more bearable and being able to stretch out helped my recovering limbs. An added bonus was watching the girls enjoying the well-appointed reclining seats, in-flight entertainment, and unlimited food, snacks, and soda.

After the Ramblers season ended, which saw us coming close to making it to the finals, I moved forward with the knee replacement procedure. Surprisingly on the day of surgery, Sariah was more nervous than I was, although she put on a brave face. Before they wheeled me out of the hospital room to prepare me for the procedure, she planted a long slow kiss to my lips and I thought if this is the last thing I experience before death then I'd enter the afterlife with a smile on my face.

Recovery was slow but I was seeing progress every day. I was used to dealing with athletes who'd suffered an injury, so I was able to extend myself some grace. I'd accepted it would take time for my body to heal. And with Sariah as my Florence Nightingale, I was a happy patient. She was always hovering nearby to fluff a pillow or apply a heating pad when the soreness kicked in. I told her not to fuss, but it was futile. So I allowed her to cosplay as the sexy nurse who administered care with two hundred and fifty milligrams of full mouth kisses as needed.

I was healthy and strong and if I continued to do the exercises and put in the work, I would be back to myself in no time. Scratch that, this surgery was supposed to make me better than I was before, and I was hopeful that would be the ultimate outcome.

After walking into the event space, the girls ditched me to mingle and take pictures with some of their favorite influencers who were in attendance. The venue was decorated almost like a spa but cozier. Every piece of décor spoke to Sariah's refined taste. I was left alone in the corner searching the party for my girlfriend. She'd left the apartment hours ago to make sure the finishing touches were completed to her specifications.

When I locked eyes with Sariah from across the room, her face lit up. She excused herself from the group she was talking to and made her way in my direction. It took a few minutes for her to get to me. It seemed like every fifth step she was stopped by someone who wanted to shmooze or a staff member that needed clarification. When she finally made it to my little corner of the world, I pulled her into an embrace, breathing in her delectable scent which almost made me salivate.

"You made it. Where are the girls?" she asked.

"I told them to stay close but they are off somewhere living their best lives, I'm sure."

"Do you need to sit? I have chairs tucked away exclusively for you so you can sit whenever you need to." She pointed to the cane in my right hand.

"I'm fine. Standing is a good thing because it helps strengthen the legs and joints."

"Well you just let me know I don't want you overexerting yourself."

"This place looks amazing and you are absolutely stunning." I placed a kiss on her bare shoulder. She wore a lavender colored dress that caressed her curves and heels, which lengthened her statuesque frame.

All eyes were on her but this beautiful woman only seemed to have eyes for me. Not going to lie, I got immense satisfaction out of being on the arm of the boss. She'd just graced the cover of *Essence* magazine in which she was touted as a beauty industry change maker and an NBA power player.

The magazine was spot on. With a little help from me, we signed Aldridge Mosley to join the Ramblers for the upcoming season. Colin Pratt wasn't happy with the acquisition, most likely because he could see the writing on the wall when it came to his future with the organization. But with Mosley on our team, I was hopeful we could secure a championship.

"I'm just glad it all came together. After this I can take a break and just enjoy the remainder of our summer."

"In less than a week we will be laid out on a beach

with paper umbrellas floating in our glasses," I reminded her.

"Yep, and I plan to spend every day of that vacation fucking you senseless," she purred.

I was on board with that. After the surgery, I was ordered to abstain from sex for a few weeks. It hadn't been easy and Sariah turned into a rodeo queen, riding my dick while I just laid back and enjoyed the view. Now that my leg was able to bare my weight for longer periods, I intended to fuck her good and proper in the upcoming days.

"I'm counting on it."

Sariah was an unexpected surprise. I never could have predicted the death of Grover Thornton would have such a profound impact on me. His passing brought Sariah into my life and saw me falling madly in love with his daughter. Words had not been invented to describe how fortuitous I was to have found her. But I planned to spend every day making her feel my love.

SARIAH

AFTER TRACIE AND I TOOK TO THE STAGE SINGING THE praises of the skincare line and thanking everyone for coming, I went in search of my people. I found the twins conspiring at a table.

"Are you two having a good time?"

"The best. We met That's Just Kassi," Jhené beamed.

Kassi Jett a.k.a. That's Just Kassi was an überpopular

influencer who'd been creating makeup videos since she was a kid.

"Was she just as nice in person as she appears online?" I asked, genuinely curious.

"She was so sweet and she told us our skin was flawless," Ebony said.

"Well I'm glad you're both having a good time. Remember to stay close by and if you need me or your dad, just ask one of the staff and they'll give me a call." I stroked their hair, which was in matching halo braids. Each had their unique style and personality, but they were adamant about wearing their hair exactly the same tonight.

Now that I was done working the room, I could just relax and enjoy the event and I wanted to do that by Justus's side. I found my man at a table talking basketball with a gentleman wearing a jacket made of fake colorful feathers. Even at a beauty event, Justus would find someone to talk shop with. Taking a seat, I listened as the two men passionately debated the upcoming season. The current season only just ended, and they were already fully invested in the possibilities of the new one.

I couldn't blame them. I was just as fanatical. Many a night, Justus and I had fallen asleep discussing our hopes for the team and our excitement about acquiring Aldridge Mosley. We were a basketball family. A smile settled on my face as I remembered when my father would make that claim and Benji and I would roll our eyes. The men finally ended their conversation with a dap and Justus's cognac eyes landed on me.

"I checked on the girls. They're doing good. They met That's Just Kassi."

"I'm not even going to pretend I know who that is."

I laughed around a yawn.

"Tired?"

"I think I'm finally coming down from the frantic last-minute push to get everything done."

With Justus, I'd been rewarded with things I didn't even know I wanted. Ebony and Jhené were bratty rays of sunshine I couldn't get enough of. I was so honored that Justus trusted me enough to invite me into their lives. Falling in love with Justus meant I also inherited a mini family with the girls and oddly enough, Melody, Justus's ex-wife, whom I enjoyed getting to know and now counted as a good friend. Nothing weird here, just a perfectly blended family all rallied around the twins. A few months ago my life flipped a fucking uey followed by a sharp left. But the final destination was a magnificent one.

I leaned into Justus's embrace. "Thank you for supporting me."

"Are you kidding? I ride hard for you in all things."

"Well I just want you to know your support is felt and greatly appreciated."

"Thank you." Justus finished the last of his champagne.

"So I was driving through the neighborhood the other day and I saw a for sale sign on a large single story home. I was wondering if you'd want to check it out when we got back to Vegas." I eyed him cautiously.

"I thought you liked your place?"

"I do but this listing has his and hers closets and extra rooms so we could both set up offices."

Justus squeezed my hand. "Are you sure this is what you want?"

"Waking up to your face every single morning? Definitely."

"I thought people were supposed to be married before moving in together," he teased.

"What can I say … I'm a rule breaker."

His mouth curved into a smile. "Not for too long. Once I get rid of this cane and I'm able to get down on one knee, I plan to stake full claim."

A chill of delight trilled over my spine. I leaned in inches from his kissable lips. "It's a date, Coach."

THANK YOU. LET'S CONNECT.

Thank you so much for reading Jump Ball. If you enjoyed Sariah & Justus's story, please help a sister out and leave a review or tell a friend. Your feedback is important to me and will help other readers decide whether to read my book too.

Feel free to connect with me virtually. I would love to engage with you.

: @authorkashathompson

: @authorkashathompson

: @authorkthompson

HAPPY READING,

Kasha

ABOUT THE AUTHOR

Kasha Thompson is a contemporary romance author. She writes authentic love stories that examine the complexity of falling and staying in love. Her books center black love with relatable characters, humor, and spice.

ALSO BY KASHA THOMPSON